JULIE

Vivian Schurfranz

SCHOLASTIC INC.
New York Toronto London Auckland Sydney

ISBN 0-590-42021-6

12 11 10 9 8 7 6 5 4 3 2 1   8 9/8 0 1 2 3/9

Printed in the U.S.A.   01

JULIE

A SUNFIRE® Book

SUNFIRE®

Chapter One

FIFTEEN-YEAR-OLD Julie Fulton, dismounting from her horse, looked up the muddy street of Crooked Branch with the purple Wasatch Mountains in the background. You'd never guess, she thought, by the makeshift wooden shanties and tents of the railroad workers that it was 1868. They appeared even more sodden and grim on such a gray November day. She sighed. How different Crooked Branch, Utah, was from Denver, Colorado! She had moved with her family from Denver only eight months ago, but it seemed as if she'd been in this ramshackle town for a lifetime!

Julie tethered her frisky black horse to a rail and patted the mare's muzzle. "I won't be long, Cinder. Only need to pick up a few things for Mother." She reached into her jeans pocket and pulled out a list.

Suddenly there was a blood-curdling yell. The saloon door burst open, and a wild-eyed man rushed out the door. A second man, bearded, and brandishing two pistols over his head, was in hot pursuit. He fired in the air and shouted, "Come here, you lowdown cheat! I saw that ace of spades up your sleeve!"

The two men were as drunk as could be at ten o'clock in the morning, Julie thought disgustedly.

The first man dashed into the street, pulling out his six-shooter and pointing at the saloon. He weaved back and forth, then pulled the trigger. A windowpane shattered.

For an instant Julie froze. These two were shooting at anything that moved! When Cinder neighed in terror, Julie spurted into action. Holding onto her floppy hat with one hand and her nose with the other, she dived into the horse trough, breaking the thin film of ice.

As the frigid water closed over her head, she held her breath and counted to ten, wondering if the two crazy gunmen had finished each other off yet. For a little settlement, Crooked Branch was more crooked than most railroad towns! Cautiously, her head broke the surface.

Blinking the moisture from her eyes, she saw the two whooping and hollering men running down the street. Standing in the horse trough, Julie watched balefully as they disappeared around a corner. All at once she heard a loud guffaw.

Splashing about in the trough, she turned and glowered at a young man. His head was thrown back, showing even white teeth that sparkled against his sun-bronzed skin.

"What are you cackling about?" she asked between clenched teeth. Glaring at him, she cast one leg over the edge to get out of the frigid water, but all at once, one foot slipped and down she went again, sinking to the slick bottom.

She tried to struggle to the surface, but before she could succeed, she felt strong hands lifting her up and setting her on the ground.

Sputtering, she pushed against this would-be rescuer, this laughing hyena's broad chest. She stood back, cocking her head to get a better view of the boy who thought she was such a joke. Brushing back the red curls plastered over her eyes, she saw a handsome young man whose black curly hair crowned his head, and whose eyes were as blue and crystal clear as the Colorado River on a sunny day. He leaned down and plucked her floating hat from the trough. "I wouldn't put this on just yet," he said with a grin, handing the dripping hat to her.

Snatching it from him, she muttered,

"Darn outlaws in this town. I've never seen so many fights and gun duels in my life!" She stood with her hands on her hips, daring him to laugh again. "Haven't you ever seen anyone *wet* before?" she asked, her voice rising.

"Oh, I've seen girls wet before," he said, sapphire glints reappearing in his amused eyes, "from the rain maybe, but not from being dunked in a horse trough!"

She slapped her hat against her leg, glowering at him, her green eyes sparking. It would give her a great deal of pleasure to shove him into the same place she'd been!

Laughing, the tall dark boy reached for her hand. "Come on, let's go inside Tucker's General Store and get you dried off!"

Despite her chattering teeth, she stammered, "I — I'm going home!"

Amazed, she watched as he stubbornly shook his head and grasped her hand.

"I'm leaving!" she said defiantly, attempting to free her wrist, but at the same time noticing from the corner of her eye a crowd beginning to gather. Julie knew she must look ridiculous with her hair plastered to her head, her fleece-lined jacket dripping water, and her boots squishing. She choked with fury. "Who do you think you are?" Her voice was loud and angry, and she heard a few titters from the onlookers.

"Why, I'm Dylan O'Kelly, best tracklayer

this side of the Rockies!" He stood with feet apart, his red-and-black checked shirt open with a red bandanna tied around his neck. "And who might you be, Missy?"

She pressed her lips together, not replying. With as much dignity as she could muster, with water streaming down her back, she stared at him coolly. But Dylan just stood there with a silly grin on his face! There was no intimidating this boy who exuded self-confidence.

"You *are* a sight!" Dylan said good-naturedly. "Come on, Missy! Inside!" he ordered firmly, shoving her ahead of him. "Unless," he lowered his head, talking quietly in her ear, "you'd rather have me carry you over my shoulder."

Her eyes flashed, but she stomped up the store steps, glancing neither to the right nor left. She was enough of a fool sight without being carried in like a sack of potatoes.

"Hi, Julie Fulton! What happened?" Hank Tucker questioned, pausing in mopping the floor, and leaning his thin frame on the mop handle.

"Julie Fulton," Dylan dutifully reported, emphasizing her name and winking at her, "dived headfirst into the horse trough."

"Why'd you go and do a crazy thing like that?" asked Hank.

"There was a shoot-out," she said defensively.

"Yup, there sure was!" Hank exclaimed. "I slammed the door so hard that three pitchers broke!"

Dylan laughed heartily. "I can still see Julie's flailing arms."

In an instant she whirled on Dylan. Then, gazing into his laughing eyes, she bit off her sharp retort and looked down at her shirt and jeans that stuck to her like a second skin. A smile tugged at the corners of her mouth. Laughter bubbled up from inside, and she giggled. She knew she must look like a soaked cat. Soon all three were laughing as Dylan moved her to the potbellied stove in the rear.

"Here, Julie," Hank said, grabbing a dress from a box. "Put this on, but be careful of it. This came all the way from Omaha!" He peered at her over his metal-rimmed spectacles. "Careful now, Julie. I don't want anything to happen to the prettiest frock in the store." Hank handed her a frayed towel for good measure.

"I'll be careful," she assured him, taking the pink ruffled dress and folding it gingerly over her arm.

Going behind the back curtains, she undressed, dried herself, and slipped into the soft chiffon. She hadn't even had a dress like this when she lived in Denver. To be truthful, she hadn't really desired one. But now that she was almost sixteen, almost grown, she'd love such a gown. She straightened the ruffled collar, wishing there was a mirror in the storeroom. If only she had someplace to wear this beauty, and if only she had a beau!

Julie fluffed out her hair, but the curls only sprang back into place like coiled springs. She knew the soft pink fabric was flattering next to her auburn hair and tanned skin, and she twirled about. Why, this was a dress similar to what Agatha Simpson, her best friend in Denver, would wear. She'd look stunning in it, too. Agatha, tall and stately, had a porcelain complexion and abundant chestnut hair that she wore in an elaborate chignon. The corners of Julie's generous mouth quirked upward. Agatha was just her opposite, Julie thought. No chiffon dress would be able to change her into another Agatha. No, the fact was that even in a beautiful dress she was still a tomboy, with unruly thick curls, freckles, a turned-up nose, and deep dimples on either side of a wide mouth.

Entering the warm storefront room, stacked high with pots and pans, shovels and picks, sugar, coffee beans, and beef jerky, she gratefully took the steaming mug of coffee that Hank handed her. Then he went back to mopping the floor. Dylan, one foot up on a pickle vat, was drinking his coffee. When he glimpsed Julie, he slowly lowered his foot, eyes widening. "I can't believe you're the same girl I fished out of the horse trough!" he exclaimed, studying her with obvious delight. "Julie," he burst out, "you're beautiful!"

Feeling her pink cheeks flame even rosier, she tried to act as if his compliment was an everyday occurrence. Casually, she draped her jeans and jacket over the shelf above the stove, but was overly conscious of her bare feet. She wiggled her toes to avoid splinters from the rough floor boards and wished she had satin slippers and silk stockings to go with her pretty dress.

Dylan pulled up a bench. "Sit down, Julie." His smile was as warm as the fire.

Daintily she sat on the bench, adjusting her skirts and feeling the stove heat radiate over her. How good it felt to be warm and dry, and to be sipping hot coffee with Dylan's eyes constantly on her. She shot him a covert glance. Why was she so concerned about Dylan? Julie asked herself. Was she trying to impress him? She had to admit she was. There was no doubt he was the handsomest boy she'd ever seen, but what she really liked about him was the humor that seemed to be lurking just beneath the surface of his dancing eyes.

"I see you're a railroad man," she stated, hoping to get him talking about himself. She wanted to learn more about this Dylan O'Kelly!

"Sure am," he said proudly, running his thumb up and down his suspender. "I'm one of the eight hundred 'Irish Terriers' that General Grenville Dodge brought in from New York City to build the Union Pacific."

"So you're Irish," Julie replied, with a smile, remembering how her father was forever praising the Irishmen's stamina and skill.

"Sure 'n I'm Irish," Dylan bragged. "Can't you tell by my brogue?"

"I was born in Denver, so I haven't met many Irish or Easterners."

"I *was* an Easterner," corrected Dylan. "But now I intend to stay out in these wide open spaces and build railroads. Why, this country is just opening up to the railroad. Sometimes I can't believe I'm part of hitching up the Union Pacific to the Central Pacific Railroad! Think of it!" His face glowed with an inner vision. "The first transcontinental railroad that will link New York to Sacramento!" He nodded knowingly. "And that's only a beginning! Soon there will be other territories to need track, and I'll be the first one there!" He sobered. "I'm saving to invest, too."

Julie laughed. "I can see you love the railroad, but you don't need to bother convincing *me*! The Fultons are a railroad family, too. My brother, Michael, is a spiker. My father is one of the chief engineers and my mother. . . ."

"Don't tell me," Dylan interrupted, holding up a calloused hand. "I just made the family connection. Why, every mulewhacker, tieman, ironman, spiker, dynamiter, tunneler, grader, shoveler, bolter, and surveyor knows your mother, Rosalind Fulton! Better known as 'Rosie.' Yes, indeed! We depend on her to tap out those telegraph messages. It would be hard to keep the supply trains coming in with our material if it weren't for her. If we're going to beat out the Central Pacific, we've got to have Rosie."

Julie beamed, proud of her mother's accomplishments. Rosie had taught her the Morse code so that she, too, was able to send out messages. Several times she had even substituted for her mother. True, there hadn't been any exciting messages that came through, but still she was sitting in the depot at the telegraph machine and she was depended upon. She was proud of her father and Michael, also. All her family had been hired by the Union Pacific Railroad, except her, of course. But one of these days she'd be a railroad woman, too! She was so excited to be part of the Union Pacific, a railroad that had started at Omaha and was now nine hundred and sixty-six miles west of that Nebraska town. It was being built at breakneck speed to cover more rail mileage than the Central Pacific, which was moving east just as rapidly from Sacramento.

"Do you think we'll beat the Central Pacific?"

"Sure 'n I do!" He answered without a moment's hesitation. "The government is going to give land and money to the railroad that lays the most track, and that's going to be us, the Union Pacific!"

"It will be hard beating Charles Crocker's Chinese workers on the Central Pacific. I've heard they're a fast lot."

"If it came between a Chinese man and an Irishman, I'd bet on the Irish every time! Old Crocker has a lot of us Irish boys working for him, too. Nope, the Union Pacific will win. You'll see!"

"I hope you're right," she replied doubtfully. "With winter and the mountains ahead of us. . . ." Her voice trailed off.

"I know I'm right!" Dylan said, taking a last gulp of coffee and emphatically setting the mug down.

For a moment she was as sure as he was. His lean body, broad shoulders, and muscled arms made it hard to imagine anyone else could win over such toughness.

"Julie," Hank said, sauntering up to them. "Do you think you're dry?" He brushed gently at the hem of the pink dress.

"Yes," she said, leaping to her feet and feeling her partially dried jeans. "My clothes are dry enough to put on. Thanks, Hank, for letting me wear this." Wistfully she looked down at the lovely dress.

"Julie," Dylan asked impulsively, "can I see you again?"

"If you'd like to," she answered, nonchalantly removing her jeans and jacket from the shelf and hoping Dylan couldn't hear her heart pounding.

"Perhaps Saturday for the Irish Festival down by the depot?"

Embarrassed, Julie didn't know what to reply, although the magnetism of his smile drew a smile from her lips.

"Saturday at four o'clock?" Dylan added hopefully.

"That will be fine," she said, whirling about and fleeing to the back room.

All the way home Julie couldn't stop humming. She remembered the many times in Denver when Agatha had gone out with boys while she had stayed home playing whist with her parents. Michael, too, was dating, but always the same girl, Liza. In fact, as soon as the railroad was finished he planned to settle in Denver and marry Liza. Maybe, Julie dreamed, she'd stay in Utah and marry Dylan. How silly I am, she snorted suddenly, grinning at such a farfetched idea. After Saturday she'd probably never see Dylan again! As she took the steps two at a time, though, she couldn't wait to tell her mother.

Chapter Two

ENTERING her family's small but comfortable house, Julie was surprised to see Michael seated at the dining room table. Why was he home in the middle of the day? And why was their mother applying a wet cloth to his forehead?

"What happened?" Julie gasped, noticing her brother's half-closed eye and his bleeding lip.

Rosalind turned her head, pressing her mouth into a thin line. "It's the Chinese and Irish! Fighting again! Forever fighting!" Her florid face flushed an even deeper red, and she agitatedly wiped her hands on her apron. "Your poor father is out there in the mountains trying to figure a pass through them. Back here there's nothing but brawling and squabbling!" Her thick brows knit together, and she pursed her full lips. "I can't understand why you were twenty-eight miles west of here, Michael." Resolutely, she poked a hairpin back into the jet black hair swirled in a bun atop her head.

"I told you, Mother. I was with a couple of graders who went ahead to check out the territory. We knew the Central Pacific advance crews would be near, and we wanted to see how much progress they'd made." He winced as Rosalind dabbed at his swollen eye. "We ran into a couple of surveyors and two Chinese workers." There was a twinkle in his good eye. "The first thing Tim O'Brien and Shawn Ryan did was to jeer at the Chinese. From then on it was every man for himself!" He laughed. "The other fellows look just as black and blue as me!"

Pointing at the enamel washbasin, Rosalind said, "Julie, hand me a clean washcloth, will you?"

Pressing the cloth against her son's bruised lip, Rosie shook her head. "Your father will be home tonight, Michael. I'd hate him to see you like this."

"Oh, it isn't that bad," Michael said, his square face breaking into a smile. "A poor Chinese worker had his leg broken."

"I declare!" Rosie exclaimed in exasperation. "We've got twenty saloon-keepers in

Crooked Branch and only one doctor! It's all backward."

"Ouch!" Michael muttered, grimacing at Rosie's touch.

"Michael, how did *you* get involved?" Julie asked, wringing out a second cloth and handing it to her mother.

"I was trying to break up a fight between a Chinese man and two burly Irishmen." He smiled ruefully, his gray eyes crinkling at the corners. "I got caught in the middle." His carrot-colored hair stood up like railroad spikes, and his battered eye was already turning a deep purple.

"Here," Julie murmured, "let me take off your boots." She busied herself pulling off first one mud-splattered boot, then the other. She and Michael had had a special relationship for as long as she could remember. Although he was four years her senior, he had been her mentor, teaching her to ride, shoot, and fish, skills that had proved very useful in this wild place. They were close, too. When she was five years old and had fallen off her horse, for instance, it was Michael who had been the first to help her up and gently coax her back in the saddle.

Standing up, Julie patted him on his broad shoulders and hung up his jacket. Her news about Saturday with Dylan was forgotten, and her buoyant feeling was replaced by a

15

sinking one. The railroad that they all loved would never be finished if this constant fighting didn't stop!

The week dragged and so did Julie's spirits. The snow had impeded a supply train coming in until the snow-catcher train came through to clear the tracks like a great beaked bird. The frozen ground was making progress almost impossible. It was said Jack and Dan Casement, brothers who supervised the construction, were fuming at the delay. The Central Pacific Railroad had been stalled by mountains, too, in the summer months, but now they had clear sailing across Nevada. It appeared that they might lay more track than the Union Pacific. Julie hoped and prayed the Union Pacific would win out over the opposing side. It would not only mean a substantial bonus for her father, but it would also mean a move back to Denver where they would build a new house. She closed her eyes. Six months ago she would have been eager to move back home, but now she was not so sure. This new untamed land was beginning to get into her blood. Lately Crooked Branch, even with all its faults, didn't look so bad.

By Friday Julie's spirits lifted in anticipation of spending Saturday with Dylan. To celebrate, she decided to go off to her favorite spot in the mountains.

As she rode Cinder up through Devil's

Mouth, she gazed down upon the trestle, a railroad bridge two hundred feet in the air that stretched fifteen hundred feet across Devil's Canyon. The trestle soared high against the clear blue sky, looking delicate and fragile as it straddled Black Mountain and the Devil's Mouth Tunnel. It always amazed Julie that such a lacelike structure could carry the heavy supply trains that thundered across. One train a day delivered ties and equipment. But soon the rails would be snowbound and it would be difficult to get a mule train through the Wasatch Mountains, let alone a locomotive.

Tethering Cinder, she moved to the footbridge built alongside the railroad trestle. The swaying bridge, with planks strung like piano keys, always gave her a thrill of danger as she carefully picked her way across, holding tightly to the ropes and balancing from side to side with the undulations. Below yawned a rocky crevice with a stream that meandered through the stony bed like a silver ribbon.

Reaching the other side, she breathed deeply. The fresh pine scent, pungent and tangy, filled her with an exhilarating aliveness. She gazed across the canyon at Crooked Branch, its grimy grayness hidden by the shimmering sunlight reflecting off the tin roofs. She turned her back on the scene and walked through the fir trees until she came

17

upon a clearing of an old construction camp. Already saplings and underbrush had taken over where once tent pegs, workers' shacks, and stacked stockpiles of rail ties had been.

Reaching a back path that snaked up the mountainside, she climbed up to the row of scrub pine trees. A snowflake or two settled on her jacket as she hiked steadily up the steep trail, stopping once to pluck a hardy snowflower.

After an hour's walk, far from any sign of civilization, she came upon a grove of cedar trees. Pausing, Julie flung up her arms. How she yearned to embrace this entire unspoiled, rugged area. Its craggy beauty and peaceful quiet were her secret haven. What a contrast, Julie thought, to Crooked Branch!

Scooping away a thin layer of snow, she sank down beneath a pine tree and leaned back. Briefly she wondered if the two Casement brothers would be given orders to clean up Crooked Branch as they'd done several years ago in Julesburg, Nebraska, which some called the "wickedest city in America."

A white rabbit scampered in front of Julie, breaking into her thoughts. She rose, shading her eyes against the pale sun. It was time to return.

Again making her way through the blueberry bushes and brambles, she slowly wended her way back, crossed the bridge, and found Cinder patiently waiting. "Come on, old girl, let's head for home. The bread has risen by now, and I promised Mother I'd put it in the oven."

Arriving home, Julie was pleased to see her father. He had gotten in early from the field and was earnestly engaged in a conversation with a young man.

She hurried in, flung her arms about his neck, and hugged him. "Welcome home, Father. When did you get in?"

There was a twinkle in his slate-gray eyes as he held her at arm's length. The creases in his ruggedly handsome face showed a deep strength. Pulling on his short gray beard, he gazed adoringly at his daughter. "About twenty minutes ago. Come over here, Julie. I want you to meet my new assistant."

She directed her attention to the young man who had been poring over a map but who was now staring at her.

"Julie," her father said, running his hand through his red hair tinged with gray. "This is Samuel Harper, an up-and-coming surveyor! Samuel, meet my daughter, Julie."

"It's a great pleasure, Miss Fulton," Samuel said, solemnly surveying *her* as he held out his hand.

She grasped his hand firmly, a sparkle in her impish eyes. With his impeccably creased trousers, silk shirt, and shiny leather boots, he no doubt disapproved of her disheveled appearance. She stepped back with a teasing grin and pulled a burr from her tangled hair. "Have you been in Crooked Branch long, Mr. Harper?"

"No, I just arrived from Washington, D.C., last Monday. I'm staying with my uncle, Hiram Harper." His well-groomed features were reserved, but his eyes never left Julie's face.

Glancing at him sharply, she asked, "Not the Hiram Harper of the Double H Stage Line?"

"One and the same," Samuel answered, his features softening in a smile that warmed his sober face. His neatly cut brown hair and aquiline nose gave him an aristocratic air.

"Doesn't your uncle feel as if he's fighting a losing battle?"

Samuel was visibly shocked. "What do you mean?"

"Well, everyone knows that once the railroad's completed there won't be any need for stagecoaches. Your uncle will be penniless."

"He hasn't mentioned it," Samuel responded stiffly.

Jay Fulton chuckled. "Hiram Harper can take care of himself, Julie. He owns land from here to California!" He clapped Samuel on the back. "The Union Pacific made this lad an offer he couldn't refuse. Samuel graduated top engineer in his class, and the railroad snapped him up, paying his transportation out here and a hefty salary to boot."

Samuel modestly studied the clapboard floor, not replying, but a tinge of pink flamed across his cheekbones.

"Well, Mr. Harper," she said cheerily. "Congratulations! You wouldn't mind if I called you Samuel, would you?"

Quickly he glanced up, and a small smile crept across his round face again. "I don't mind at all, Miss Fulton," he politely replied.

"Call me Julie."

"J-Julie," he stammered.

Turning to her father, she asked, "Father, after I've put the bread in the oven would you mind if I sat by the fire and read?"

"Not at all, darling." He held up an admonishing finger. "But you'll need to keep quiet."

"I think I can manage that for about ten minutes." She laughed, leaving them alone.

When she returned, their heads were bent low over a large topography map, and they were murmuring about the best route for new track, whether through Bear's Head Pass or the Green River Trail.

Julie stretched out contentedly on her stomach before the stone fireplace with its yellow dancing flames. She opened her Greek mythology book, flipping through the pages until she came to her favorite myth — the story of Antigone, and how the brave girl defied the State. Every once in a while she glanced up, only to catch Samuel staring at her. He seemed embarrassed, hastily averting his eyes, and studiously examining the map again.

Julie turned the page, but she was no longer reading. Samuel Harper intrigued her. He was handsome, naive, intelligent, and obviously interested in her. She wanted to know more about him. And she would, too. Giving him a sidelong glance, she studied his strong profile. Yes, he was good-looking, but he didn't have the dark, flashing appeal of Dylan.

She sighed happily, rolling over on her back. Tomorrow she and Dylan would attend the Irish Festival. What fun it would be! How could she even think of anyone else?

Late the next afternoon, Samuel Harper was forgotten when Dylan knocked on the door. As Julie ran downstairs, she felt pretty in her rust-colored dress, the same shade as her abundant hair, which she had caught at the nape of her neck with a turquoise ribbon. Beneath her circular skirt peeked the tips of black high-topped shoes, just ready for dancing.

Opening the door, Julie greeted Dylan, who stood leaning against the door jamb with a grin on his face. "How are you, Miss Julie Fulton? Ready to do the Irish jig?" He pulled on his jacket and did a quick little sidestep.

"I'm ready," she answered with a chuckle. "Come in while I put on my cape."

"First," he said, grabbing her arm, "here's a small gift for you." He held up a tiny Irish shamrock, dangling from a silver chain. "I didn't bring you flowers, but I wondered if you'll accept a wee Irish charm instead?"

The dainty three-leaf clover caught the light as it changed from emerald to jade green. "Oh, I love it!" she exclaimed, almost clapping her hands.

"Here, let me fasten it about your neck," he offered.

Happily, Julie turned around. His hand softly touched her throat and then the necklace was secure. Quickly she spun about to face him, patting the charm. "How does it look?"

"Perfect!" His blue eyes shone. "You must have a touch of green for the Irish Festival, Julie." His finger lifted her chin. "The charm matches the deep green of your eyes."

She smiled and said, "Blarney slips so easily over your silver-coated tongue, Mr. O'Kelly." Laughing, she confessed, "But I enjoy it."

Reaching for her cape, she flung it over her shoulders, and they left hand in hand.

"My parents are already at the Festival," Julie said. "Mother baked soda bread, and Father is preparing a short speech to introduce Jack Casement." The cold air fanned

her warm cheeks. "I can't wait to get there."
She looked down Main Street. Everyone in
town seemed headed for the Community
Hall.

Dylan's hand tightened on her gloved
fingers. "We'll have fun dancing. I'll have
the prettiest colleen there!"

She glowed at his compliment, and when
they entered the hall, her mood matched the
merriness around her. The rafters were
festooned with green and white ribbons, and
the fiddler was plucking on a few strings.

"Excuse me, Julie," Dylan said in a con-
spiratorial whisper, "but I'm needed back-
stage."

"Oh?" she said, her brows arching. "What
are you up to?"

"You'll see." He grinned, his teeth flashing
white against his dark skin. "You'll see soon
enough," he repeated gleefully, bounding up
on the platform and disappearing behind the
curtains.

Moving to the punch bowl, Julie noticed the
green froth and the small cups, but before she
could use the ladle to scoop out a cupful,
Samuel was at her side, handing her a cup.

"Why, thank you, Samuel," she said,
standing on tiptoe and peering over his
shoulder.

He smiled, brown eyes shimmering with
golden flecks. "There's no one with me if

that's what you're looking for. Are you alone, too, Julie?"

"I-I'm with someone," she stammered, wondering why she was so flustered.

Suddenly the fiddlers struck up a lively tune, and Dylan, along with three other Irish Terriers dressed in short green jackets, tall hats with a buckle in front, short pants, and buckled shoes, came on stage. They broke into a spritely Irish clog dance, their shoes resounding loudly on the heavy oak platform. Faster and faster their feet flew, and soon their hands were keeping time to the music, hitting first their hips and then the soles of their shoes.

Julie loved the cloggers and clapped until her hands were red. When Dylan joined her, she said jubilantly, "Your dancing was marvelous!"

Dylan, an amused smile playing about his lips, said softly, "Ah, Julie, if you could see your smile in the candlelight."

A flush crept like a shadow over her cheeks, and she changed the subject. "You're such a good dancer, Dylan. I didn't know you had so much talent!"

"More talent than you realize," he said with a wink. "Even talented enough to fish young girls out of horse troughs!"

"Don't remind me," she said, laughing.

"Horse troughs?" Samuel asked, coming up behind her.

"Oh, Samuel," she said, rolling her eyes. "It's a long story. I'll tell you one of these days." She took his arm. "Samuel, I'd like you to meet Dylan O'Kelly. Dylan, this is Samuel Harper, my father's new assistant."

"New assistant, is it?" Dylan commented. "One of the surveyors from back East?"

"Washington, D.C.," Samuel said shortly.

"Well, Mister, you plan out the route, and we'll lay the track as neat as a hem stitch."

"Don't worry," Samuel said seriously. "We'll find the best route possible."

"That's dandy," Dylan said, jauntily cocking his black head to one side, "but right now me and my girl have an overdue dance." Lightly he took her hand, and before she knew it he had whisked her out onto the floor.

A twinge tweaked her conscience when she noticed Samuel forlornly watching from the sidelines, but she soon gave herself up to Dylan's exuberance and the jolly squawking of the fiddlers.

hind the construction train was a supply train loaded with thousands of rails, ties, spikes, switch stands, and fishplates that bolted the rails together.

Following the tracks, Julie slowed Cinder to a canter. Construction crews, wielding their pickaxes and sledge hammers, rang out their blows like an anvil chorus on the cold morning air. The hammer strokes were punctuated by grunts as the men tried to penetrate the frozen clay and sandstone, which was as hard as granite.

A crew member, standing before a roaring fire drinking coffee, shouted her name as she rode sedately by. She held up her hand in greeting, searching for Dylan among their ranks. But he was nowhere to be seen.

Riding through Red Gorge, Julie grasped Cinder's reins tightly when an explosion ripped through the rocky peak ahead. The tunnelers were blasting again. A few falling stones tumbled onto the path, causing a skittish Cinder to dance nervously to one side. The earth trembled for an instant, then silence and snowdust settled over the valley. The men were using more and more nitroglycerine explosives, but their progress had slowed to a foot or less a day. She thought grimly of the winter months ahead. The Eastern newspapers wouldn't be issuing their daily bulletin as they'd done last summer — bulletins that told of remarkable progress:

- 1 $9/10$ miles of track laid yesterday on the Union Pacific.
- 2 miles of track laid yesterday on the Union Pacific.
- $2\frac{3}{4}$ miles of track laid yesterday on the Union Pacific.

The Union Pacific had captured the country's imagination, and people couldn't hear enough about how it and the Central Pacific Railroad would soon merge. Well, if she knew her father and the brawny Irishmen, like Dylan, they'd more than make up for lost time when the spring thaws arrived.

Right now she had more immediate problems. Unaccustomed to riding sidesaddle, she shrugged her shoulders uncomfortably. Nonetheless, she was determined to make a good impression and to look like a lady when she presented herself to Samuel. She knew he'd be pleased to see the picnic hamper, tied behind the saddle, containing fried chicken and apple pie.

Most surveyors were ordered to work in pairs in case of an Indian or outlaw attack, but she knew Samuel was working alone, surveying Two Flats. She couldn't forget the woebegone expression on his face the night of the dance. Since then he had asked her several times if she wouldn't ride out to his surveying site, but something always interfered. She smiled mischievously. Usually Dylan! Today, though, she resolved to get to know Samuel a little better. He was far from home and didn't have as many friends as Dylan. Living with his uncle must be lonely for Samuel, and his surveying job was an isolated one, for he had to keep far in advance of the other workers.

As she passed a party of graders, smoothing the way for more track to be laid, she greeted their calls with a friendly wave and kept riding.

Arriving at Two Flats, she glimpsed Samuel pacing off the distance between two large boulders.

"Samuel! Hello!" she shouted.

He paused, then waved enthusiastically. "Julie!" He ran to meet her, grabbing Cinder's reins and looking up at her with a smile. "This is an unexpected pleasure. I didn't think you were ever going to take me up on my invitation." His nut-brown eyes deepened. "There could be danger out here, though. About an hour ago I saw a Cheyenne hunting party."

"Indians?" she questioned, her eyes widening with pretended fright. "And I brought such a nice lunch."

He helped her down, and she slid gracefully into his arms. "You look lovely today, Julie," he said softly.

"Why, thank you, Samuel." Their eyes locked, and for a moment she thought he was going to kiss her, but instead he hastily released her, moving away.

"I suppose," he said, swallowing hard, "that we could eat in that rocky niche over there." He pointed to a promontory surrounded by pine trees. "Then," he said, "I'd better take you home."

"I hope I won't interfere with your work," she said innocently, knowing full well that was exactly what she was doing.

"I'll be glad to call it a day. I've been working seven days a week trying to do as much surveying as I can before we're holed up for the winter." He took her hand, leading her to the picnic site.

The rocks were a good protection against the cold, and the cavelike structure was cozy as they huddled together out of the wind.

As Julie unpacked the lunch, she said, "Tell me about yourself, Samuel. Do you have any brothers or sisters?"

"One married sister who lives in New York and a younger brother, Todd." A spark warmed his eyes. "Todd really wanted to come West with me, but he needs to stay in the seventh grade." He paused. "Besides, I don't think Uncle Hiram could put up with the little scamp."

"I'd like to meet him," she said sincerely.

"Todd's very different from me when I was his age," Samuel said, taking a bite from a chicken leg. "He plays baseball and tennis. *I* used to read. Read everything I could get my hands on."

So this was Samuel, she thought. He must have gotten used to being alone when he was growing up. "And your father?" she asked gently, more to change the subject than for information. "Is he a surveyor, too?"

Sam shook his head, lacing his fingers about his knee. "No, he's an architect, and Mother helps run his office." His face turned solemn, and he said wistfully, "I miss them."

There was an undercurrent of amusement in her voice when she said, "They sound as if they might miss you, too, Samuel."

He nodded, smiling. "According to their last letter, they do."

"Will you go back to your family in Washington when the railroad is completed?"

"I'm not sure. I might stay out West because that's where the opportunities are." He shrugged. "But I prefer the East."

For some reason his reply disappointed her, but she didn't let him see it as she tucked a wisp of hair back under her hat.

After Samuel finished his chicken, he helped himself to a slab of apple pie. "And you, Julie? What do you like to do?"

"Oh, I like to ride and sh — " She stopped herself from saying "shoot," and quickly substituted, "needlepoint. But the thing I love the most is helping Mother at the telegraph office. It makes me feel useful, and the engineers depend on us."

They chatted about the railroad, the upcoming winter, and about themselves. She was glad she'd come out here today. Samuel seemed genuinely glad to see her, and he was so easy to talk to.

Suddenly Sam jumped up. "I need to get you back to town. I'd never forgive myself if anything happened to you."

"Very well," she said demurely. She knew she could take care of herself, but Samuel viewed himself as her protector. Today she rather enjoyed being treated like a delicate flower.

Arriving safely in Crooked Branch, Julie tethered Cinder to the horse rail. The first person she saw was Dylan! Her heart plummeted as she watched him sprint down the steps of Hank's General Store. He had his hands in his pockets, and his upturned jacket collar framed his lean face. When he spied them, he said easily, "Hello, you two." The wind ruffled his black curls as he stepped closer, giving Cinder's nose a friendly pat, and giving Julie a thoughtful look. "What's my girl Julie been up to?"

Julie wasn't sure she liked it when Dylan sounded so possessive, and yet she wondered how he'd feel to learn that she'd been out with Samuel. She bit her lip, not replying. However, when Dylan noticed the picnic hamper, a slight frown clouded his eyes. She had to admit she was secretly pleased.

"Julie came out to Two Flats, and I'm escorting her home," explained Samuel. "It's not safe out there." He didn't appear at all surprised by Dylan's reference to her as "my girl."

Dylan moved closer, staring at her intently, his bright eyes darkening to a storm-blue. "Samuel's right, you know," he said evenly. "If I were you, I wouldn't go out to Two Flats alone again."

"Oh, wouldn't you?" she asked sweetly. "I'm not afraid of Indians," she paused, "or for that matter, Irishmen, either."

All at once Dylan's mouth twisted wryly. "You're not afraid of anything, Julie." He gave her a mock salute. "I'll see you tonight," he said airily, striding away with a whistle on his lips.

She sucked in her breath. She'd almost forgotten that she'd invited Dylan over for a taffy pull. Dismounting, she scarcely glanced at Samuel. What must he think of her? He no doubt thought she was a brazen girl who planned a picnic lunch with one boy in the daytime and a taffy pull with another the same night.

Samuel, however, didn't seem to mind. Taking her arm, he said good-naturedly, "After such a good lunch, Julie, the least I can do is buy you a sarsaparilla."

Going up the steps and looking at Samuel, who smiled down at her, Julie's emotions were in a turmoil. What had happened to the devil-may-care Julie who a month ago could only think of her telegraph lessons and riding? Now, suddenly, she was juggling two young men, flirting shamelessly, and pretending to be a demure young woman. She shook her red hair derisively at her new image.

Startled, Samuel shot her a quick glance. "Is something wrong, Julie?"

"Oh, no," she answered, not wanting to ruin his ideas about her. Daintily, she lifted her skirts and moved carefully up the steps. Last week she would have been dressed in jeans and would have darted up the steps two at a time. "I was just thinking of all the different roles we have to play with different people."

An arched eyebrow indicated Samuel's amused surprise. He laughed. "You're quite the philosopher, Julie."

"Yes," she murmured. "I guess so." She sighed, wondering who the true Julie really was!

Chapter Four

On Tuesday Julie rode out to meet Samuel because he had asked her to accompany him to meet his uncle. She had the uneasy suspicion Samuel was falling in love with her, and she knew she wasn't ready for that. He was attractive and always the gentleman, but he couldn't compare to Dylan. She frowned. Lately Dylan had been pushed into the background. The crew was not only working long hours, but Saturdays and Sundays as well, to lay as much track as possible before the heavy snows.

Then, too, Jack and Dan Casement were constantly tempting their workers with new incentives. In the beginning, if the men laid one mile of track a day, they received a pound of tobacco. Later, if they laid one and one-half miles of track between sunup and sundown, they were paid three dollars a day instead of the customary two. Now the Casements expected four miles of track a day and promised to pay four dollars. The workers labored long and weary hours, but who could pass up wages like that?

In the distance, Julie heard the men singing in time to the track boss's command of "Down!" every thirty seconds as the track layers dropped the rails into place. She couldn't hear the words to their song, but she knew by the rhythm what they were singing. Silently she sang the words:

> Drill, ye tarriers, drill,
> Drill ye tarriers, drill.
> Oh, it's work all day
> No sugar in your tay,
> Working on the U. Pay ra-ailway!

She could see an image of Dylan, dressed in his fleece-lined vest and corduroy trousers, lustily singing as he swung his heavy sledgehammer down on the rail tie. She missed seeing him but knew that with the oncoming winter he'd have plenty of time on his hands, and hopefully, time for her.

Then her thoughts focused on Samuel. Her father certainly spoke highly of him and the meticulous surveys he plotted. Although she enjoyed being with Samuel, she wasn't too eager to be introduced to his uncle. The rumor was that Hiram Harper was fighting every inch of rail track laid. In fact, he had just returned from a trip to Washington, D.C., where he had met with President-elect Ulysses Grant to argue that the railroad's progress was not worth the effort expended — in money and lives.

She shook her head. Now, more than ever, after the end of the bloody Civil War only three years ago, the country needed to be brought together. How could an intelligent man like Hiram Harper fail to see the importance of the transcontinental railroad? A knowing smile crossed Julie's lips. Mr. Harper's motives for fighting the railroad weren't too difficult to understand. The Double H Stagecoach Line would go bankrupt if the railroad went through!

Julie shivered in her attractive riding habit. The snug-fitting bodice was too thin for such a bone-chilling day. Her sheepskin jacket would have been much more sensible, but Samuel liked her to act the lady, and she intended to look like one, too. With her riding crop she tapped the crown of her silk top hat, which was cocked over one eye. She knew she looked like a pretty English aristocrat with the muslin veil fastened around the base, trailing down her back almost to her waist.

Digging in her heels, she urged Cinder into a gallop, wanting to reach Samuel before noon. Out past Stormy Creek and into the rocky terrain of Butte Mountain, Julie sped until she came to Stony Point.

Reaching a small rise, she saw someone below and reined in Cinder to get a better view. Suddenly she froze. Indians! Horrified, she watched as three Cheyenne Indians stacked tie rails on top of one another. Already there were three bonfires blazing. Julie knew the Cheyenne had torn up track at Logan's Gully, but she had no idea they were now starting to destroy stockpiles of rail ties as well. She felt sorry for the Indians, for the railroad would change their way of life, depending on the buffalo the way they did. Wherever the railroad went through, herds were soon depleted. Nonetheless, someone had to stop these Cheyenne before they set fire to yet another pile of ties.

All at once she was startled to see Samuel standing atop a flat-topped ledge. Jumping down, he dashed toward the Indians, yelling, "Get out of here!" His face was flushed an angry red, and he wildly waved his surveyor's rod.

An Indian, wearing black-painted stripes on his cheeks and bearing a lance, let out a war whoop and advanced toward Samuel. Samuel stood his ground and poked at the Indian when he came within reach. A second

Indian in a distinctive purple-and-white feathered war bonnet, crept up behind Sam, and with his rifle butt, hit him a glancing blow on the side of the head.

Knocked to the ground, Samuel, with a dogged shake of his head, scrambled to his feet. "This is Union Pacific property!" he thundered indignantly. Then, undaunted, he rushed the closest Indian, shoving him to the ground.

Was Samuel crazy? she thought. Didn't he realize he was outnumbered three to one? He might be killed. Flinging her fancy hat to the ground, Julie let her abundant hair tumble about her shoulders, then pulling a pistol from the saddlebag, she determinedly gritted her teeth and drummed her heels into Cinder's flanks. Her little mare leaped forward. Galloping toward the Indians, Julie cracked her whip, but Cinder was already going full tilt. Julie hollered and whooped, her voice reverberating off the canyon walls. Firing her gun in the air, she came at them like a screaming banshee.

One surprised Indian dropped a rail tie, made a running side-leap for his pony, and fled. The other two quickly followed suit.

Still shooting, Julie watched the Indian ponies kicking up the gravel dust as they raced off toward the distant foothills. Then she lowered her gun and plunged it back into the leather pouch.

Open-mouthed, Samuel observed Julie as she jumped off Cinder's back. "Samuel, are you all right?" she asked breathlessly.

"I'm all right," he repeated, with utter disbelief written all over his face. "Where did you learn to ride and shoot like that?"

"My brother, Michael," she answered, realizing her delicate-lady image had been permanently shattered.

"Well, I'm glad you came when you did," he said evenly. "I'm just relieved you weren't hurt, Julie."

"Oh, I'm fine," she replied breezily as if she did this sort of thing everyday, but the puzzled look on Samuel's face hurt. Especially since she'd just saved his life!

"You've certainly kept your skills a secret," Samuel said pleasantly, with a cool smile. He dusted off his neatly creased trousers while his brown wavy hair blew in the breeze. "Shall we head for the Double H station? My uncle will be waiting."

"Let's go," she answered with a sinking heart. His displeasure with her unladylike behavior was obvious.

As they rode to the stagecoach station, she caught Sam glancing at her warily from time to time. Even retrieving her handsome hat and setting it at a jaunty tilt didn't seem to help the image he now had of her.

They rode in silence. Julie could scarcely swallow away her disappointment at

41

Samuel's reaction. She felt as exposed as the blueberry bushes whose branches were picked clean. Now, at least, she would no longer have to pretend.

Julie kept thinking of Agatha Simpson. *She* was the type of girl for Samuel. Agatha's manners were always impeccably correct, and her demeanor was that of a well-bred lady. Even if Julie *wanted* to appear the lady, she thought, how could she, with her unruly red hair flying about her freckled face like a bramble bush? She'd always be a tomboy, no matter *who* asked her to change!

They rode past the stunted pine trees until they reached the flats beyond Butte Mountain. There, nestled in Blue Valley, was the Double H line, and in front of the station was a team of six horses harnessed to the westbound stagecoach. The driver, wearing the usual yellow kid gloves, climbed up on the high seat of the Concord wagon, and with a flick of the reins, the horses headed for the snakelike pass through the mountains.

"Come, Julie," Samuel said with a smile. "I've told my uncle a lot about you, and he's eager to meet you."

Following Samuel's horse, Julie urged Cinder carefully down the trail to the sprawling station.

Entering the station, Julie smelled horse leather and fresh hay. Hiram Harper's snow-white head was bent over a ledger, but when he saw them he immediately rose to his feet. He was a big man with a barrel chest and broad shoulders. His bushy white brows lifted in surprise as he glanced from his nephew to Julie. "Samuel, my boy," he boomed heartily, baring long even teeth, "is this the famous Julie you've been telling me about?"

Samuel took Julie's hand. "Yes, Uncle Hiram, this is Julie Fulton."

"I'm charmed, my dear."

"Thank you, sir," she replied, looking straight into his watery blue eyes. No longer would she demurely lower her eyes when complimented by a man. Samuel had discovered the real Julie, so from now on, she would not pretend!

"She may *look* like a lady, Uncle Hiram, but you should see her ride and shoot." He squeezed her hand. "She frightened away three Cheyenne Indians that were burning rail ties."

Julie smiled at Samuel's seeming forgiveness, but inwardly she wondered why he didn't mention the danger he'd been in. No doubt he wanted to forget about the incident.

"You should have left the Indians to their burning," Hiram said with a low laugh. "As you can see, Julie, I'm no friend of the railroad. Not many stagecoach men are!" He confronted her. "Julie, your family is quite well known in Crooked Branch for their work on the railroad. Tell me, how do you like our wild little town?"

She smiled sweetly, enunciating her words for Samuel's benefit. "I like it more every day. Being from Denver, I'm already used to mountains and the rough ways of the West."

Hiram shrewdly appraised Julie's top hat and riding costume. "I'm sure you can hold your own in tough situations."

She grinned, giving Samuel a sidelong glance. "Yes, I can take care of myself."

"Hmm," Hiram said, his brows moving upward again. "You've picked a lovely flower in Julie, Samuel. A wild flower, beautiful and strong."

"Yes, she has pluck," Sam admitted, then abruptly changed the subject. "Did we interrupt your bookkeeping, Uncle?"

Hiram held up his hands. "No, no. I just finished. My accounts show a tidy profit for November, but," he said, pursing his lips, "I've got most of my money tied up in twenty-three coaches and ninety horses."

Then he flung his arm around Samuel's shoulder. "Too bad the Union Pacific hired you, my boy. I hate to see you help the railroad's progress at your dear old uncle's expense. You know, if the Indians stop the railroad and Congress cuts off the money, there won't be much future out here for you, Sam. I'd hate to see you hurt." His tone was solicitous, almost patronizing.

"It would be difficult to stop the railroad now," Julie put in clearly. "I've never seen such determined workers."

Hiram's massive head swung around. "Make no mistake, Julie. This is no game." His eyes glittered with angry sapphire sparks. "The railroad can be stopped. I know your family is employed by the Union Pacific, but I just returned from Washington, D.C., and there are many powerful senators who are disgruntled with the funds that have been wasted on such a harebrained project. A cross-country railroad indeed!" His voice became louder. "Do you realize how much the government has invested in this railroad? Why, Congress pays sixteen thousand dollars a mile for track laid on prairie and three times as much for a mile of track through mountains. How long do you think they can pour in that kind of money?"

His arm tightened around Samuel's shoulders. "Yes, Sam, you'd better wake up. The sooner you return to Washington, the sooner you'll get a safer, more stable position." He gave a quick, sharp laugh. "Not that I don't want you with me, Nephew, but you must do what's best for your career."

Julie felt her neck hairs rise. Why, Hiram Harper was actually advising Samuel to quit and go back home!

"Uncle," Samuel said levelly, "I've come

this far and if the railroad can hold on until spring, we'll finish the job!"

"But the money is running out," Hiram persisted. "Your career will be made in the East, my boy." He turned his sunken eyes on hers. "Don't you agree, Julie?" he said softly. His amused look seemed to say silently, "Agree, agree!"

But she couldn't agree. She had to speak her mind. "No, I don't agree," she said firmly. "I think the railroad is going through."

Hiram Harper's amusement changed to a hard glare and all at once Julie felt a soft feather of fear tingle along her spine. She had made an enemy of Hiram Harper and it wasn't a comfortable thought.

Samuel smoothly intervened. "I'll stay until we meet the Central Pacific. I made up my mind a long time ago to stick with the Union Pacific." He moved away, straightening his shoulders, resolutely facing his uncle.

Julie knew that what Samuel had said took courage, and she smiled. At that moment she was proud of Samuel. Very proud.

Chapter Five

JULIE was glad to return home, for although Samuel was cordial, he was not his usual, charming self. She knew that her daring ride and pistol-shooting still rankled him, and that the visit with Hiram had been upsetting.

Removing her hat, she placed it on the hall stand. Was that a noise she heard? She looked up the staircase. "Mother?" she called, wondering why Rosie would be home at this time of day.

"Yes, dear," her mother answered. "Come upstairs."

Julie's eyes widened when she saw her mother's half-packed valise on the huge oak bed. "Where are you going?" she asked hesitantly.

"I'm taking the empty supply train to Cheyenne, and from there I'll go to Denver." Gently she put a hand on Julie's arm. "I just received a telegraph message this morning that your Granny Ruth is very ill. I must leave at once."

Julie's heartbeat quickened. "How sick is she?"

"Very sick, I'm afraid. It's diphtheria." Rosie folded her blue gingham dress, placing it on top, and closed the velour bag. She straightened the taffeta overskirt, caught up by interior fastenings, over her navy velvet dress. Her black hair, done in a chignon and covered by a net, gleamed richly in the soft gray light. She examined her daughter's face with red-rimmed eyes that indicated private weeping. "You'll need to take my shift at the telegraph office while I'm gone. Will you do that for me, Julie?"

"Oh, yes, Mother," she breathed, giving her a hug. "Don't worry about a thing!" It was sad to imagine her small, feisty granny lying in bed with a disease that closed off the throat and made it almost impossible to breathe.

"Frank will take the afternoon shift, and the office is closed at night, so you'll be depended upon, Julie." She patted her cheek. "I know you can handle it."

Her sadness lifted a bit at the thought of

taking over Mother's telegraph post. She loved that job!

"I know the Morse code, thanks to you. I'll be fine, Mother." She smiled. "I'll keep the trains rolling."

"I knew I could count on you!" Rosie pressed Julie's hand. "It's time to go. The train won't wait." She reached for her small-brimmed felt hat and perched it over one eye.

How lovely her mother looked, Julie thought — like a young girl. Well, after all, she was only thirty-eight and looked ten years younger. If only she could be as competent and efficient as her mother. She longed to be as highly esteemed and loved by the railroad workers as Rosie.

"Now, Julie," her mother said, "the stew is simmering over the fire for dinner tonight. Your father won't be home until tomorrow." She glanced out the window. "By the looks of this bleak sky, I'd say once he gets back to Crooked Branch he might not be able to leave for several months. It's a good thing I can still get out of town before the snow comes." She held out her arms. "Give me a kiss, Julie, and say a prayer for Granny."

"I will," she promised softly, wishing there was something *she* could do for her Granny Ruth.

After her mother had gone, Julie hauled in wood for the stone fireplace, then poked up the fire. Of all the rooms in the house, the kitchen was her favorite. The round table with its red-and-white-checked tablecloth, placed near the cheery flames, was already set with two brightly lacquered tin plates. Mother had been usual, efficient self before she left, leaving everything in order.

Pushing aside a hanging string of dried peppers, pumpkin rings, and apples, Julie lifted the lid of the iron kettle hanging from a pothook above the fire. She stirred the hearty, bubbling stew, its scent wafting throughout the kitchen. Then she sat in the rocker before the fire, enjoying the warm glow the orange and red flames cast over the room from the top rafters to the braided rug on the wooden floor.

As she watched the sparks shoot up the chimney-throat, she thought about how much her life had changed in Crooked Branch in only eight months. She missed Agatha, who she had confided in and laughed with. Every girl should have a special girl friend, no matter how far away. She exhaled a long deep breath. There were no girls her own age in Crooked Branch. In fact, girls of any age were scarce.

She leaned back, rocking to and fro. But now she had someone new. *Two* someones!

Dylan and Samuel. A log shifted, and the red blaze gleamed on the white-washed walls. For a moment she saw the image of Samuel, but his gentle face soon gave way to another image. Dylan's white teeth shone against his tanned skin, and a black curl fell over his forehead. She missed him! She hadn't even caught a glimpse of him for over a week.

The fire crackled. Through the window-pane she could see a few snowflakes, large and lacy, drifting to the ground and whitening it. In the distance she heard the train's whistle. Mother was leaving and probably wouldn't be back until spring.

Rising, Julie moved to the cupboard and took down the coffee grinder. After she had ground the coffee for supper, she gathered five apples from the bushel basket, peeling and coring them.

Suddenly the door was flung open. There stood Michael. Her heart leaped. Was her imagination still playing tricks on her? No, there was Dylan by her brother's side.

"Hello, Julie. Can we set another plate for supper?" Michael asked, brushing snow off his jacket.

"Of course," she answered eagerly, delighted to see Dylan. Her cheeks reddened as their eyes met.

"How are you?" Dylan questioned softly. "It's been too long, hasn't it?"

She nodded numbly and felt unable to speak. Why didn't she greet him in her usual breezy style? All at once she was shy and her palms dampened. Was this a normal reaction to a boy?

Dylan chuckled. "Mmmm, something smells good!" He sauntered to the fireplace, warming his hands before the fire. His stance emphasized his easy, confident manner while his bright red shirt and black trousers made him look lean and tall.

"The snow is supposed to last all night," Dylan said. "There'll be no more work on the railroad if that's the case." He cast a grin in her direction. "What about going ice skating on Green Lake tomorrow? It's frozen solid."

"I'd love to," she answered quickly, too quickly. Why couldn't she be more reserved instead of leaping in and appearing so eager?

"That's my girl," laughed Dylan.

"I'm going upstairs for a short nap before supper," Michael said, then over his shoulder he called, "Give Dylan a cup of cider."

Julie poured the amber liquid into a pewter mug, but when she handed it to Dylan he set it aside and took her in his arms. She snuggled against him easily.

Gently he lifted her chin and bent to kiss her. She leaned against him, loving his nearness. His scent of snow and cedar filled her senses. Closing her eyes, Julie felt almost dizzy as his fingers trailed down her cheek.

"Ah, my sweet colleen," he whispered. "You're the only girl for me!"

Her heart sang at his words as she nestled her head more deeply into the soft flannel of his shirt.

His arm tightened around her and she lifted her face expectantly for another kiss. But instead, Dylan abruptly released her. Reaching for the cider, he took a deep draught, then set it down. His blue eyes darkened to a smoky indigo and he said huskily, "I love you, Julie." Suddenly he grasped her hand. "When the railroad is finished, will you marry me?"

Her thick lashes flew up. Marry Dylan! Did her ears correctly hear his words? Was this really happening to Julie Fulton? "I-I don't know," she said in a small voice. "My parents. . . ."

Dylan cut the air with his hand. "I know I'll need your father's permission, but that will come later. What do you think, me darling?"

She wheeled about, staring into the flames. Her fingers instinctively clutched the shamrock charm that hung around her neck.

Dylan, coming up behind her, placed his hands on her arms. "What is it?"

She couldn't answer. His proposal had made her tongue-tied.

"It couldn't be Samuel Harper who's making you hesitate, could it?" Dylan said evenly.

"No, no, it isn't anyone." Was *this* the moment she'd waited for? She swallowed hard. Was she ready to be Dylan's wife? Was she ready to be anyone's wife? That would be a big responsibility. Then she straightened her shoulders. She could carry any responsibility.

Dylan's hand touched her hair. Turning her about to face him, he grinned down at her. "Don't be so solemn, little one. Our wedding will be a long way down the tracks." He stepped back, placing his hands on his hips, his blue eyes sparkling as he studied her.

His amused look annoyed Julie. "I don't intend to commit myself to anyone just yet," she said quickly in a voice that sounded almost defiant. But inside she was wondering how she could be saying this to Dylan. Nonetheless she mustn't rush into anything. She was only fifteen and marriage was for a lifetime!

Dylan pushed back an unruly lock of her hair, and as if reading her thoughts, he said, teasing laughter in his eyes, "You'll be sixteen in March, Julie. My mother was married at sixteen."

"And mine was married at eighteen," she countered, boldly meeting his eyes.

He threw back his head and laughed. "Don't worry, darling. I won't pressure you, but one of these days I'll sweep you off your feet and you'll remember today. You'll rush into my arms and say 'Yes, yes, I'll marry you, Dylan.' " He sobered. "You'll even forget about Samuel Harper."

"Samuel is only a good friend," she responded sharply.

"Like me?"

"Like you," she added teasingly, an impish smile spreading across her face. She touched his nose with her forefinger. "A very good friend. Now," she said, grabbing his hand, "Come and help me cinnamon and sugar the apples!"

As they moved to the table, the easy pleasure of being together returned, but Julie couldn't help wondering if she had done the right thing by putting Dylan off. Then she smiled. Knowing Dylan, he wouldn't be put off for long.

Chapter Six

IN December it snowed for five straight days, piling drifts up to fifty feet. The railroad workers joked that they could get a clean shave just by poking their faces out in the wind. Four locomotives were needed to push one snowplow, and what work was accomplished on the rails was done by men who had to toil in heavy overcoats all day, depending on shovel crews in front of them.

Now it was the Union Pacific's turn to suffer through a mountain winter. The Central Pacific had had its share of snow and delay when crossing the rugged Sierras. Durant, one of the chief engineers of the Union Pacific, was constantly pushing his men to greater speeds, but it was impossible. No longer could they make their four- or five-mile spurts of progress. They were lucky if they achieved a hundred feet a day. Besides, the precious rail ties that were brought in at $1.75 apiece were being burned by the workers to keep warm.

In the mornings the streets of Crooked Branch were empty of life, and when the wind whipped across the town, the only movement was an occasional dead branch tumbling across the shifting snow. Later in the day men would emerge from their huts and scuttle to one of the many saloons for an Irish whiskey and a poker game.

Every morning Julie trudged through snowbanks to the telegraph office. She dared not miss a day, for she knew how much men depended on the telegraph to keep supplies arriving. At least the cold, blustery weather meant that Crooked Branch would remain a railroad town for another few months. Not like Benton, Wyoming, which someone said "grew in a day and vanished in a night, but was red hot while it lasted."

General Dodge had gone on ahead to Salt Lake City to talk to Brigham Young about the pay train. It was late again, and the men were grumbling about money. Mormon graders received three dollars a day and a man and his ox team ten dollars a day plus his keep. Now more Mormon workers were needed for grading, but Mr. Young had shrewdly written into their contracts that they'd get at least eighty percent of their pay every month, or they wouldn't work. This was more than the Irish laborers received. Already they had waited two months for the gold and silver shipment.

On the way home from her morning shift at the telegraph office, the snow crunched under Julie's boots. The air was biting cold, making her cheeks red. She was looking forward to this evening, for Dylan was coming to visit and she had a special Irish dinner planned. Boiled beef and cabbage. Dylan would like that.

Since that day last month when Dylan had asked her to marry him, he'd never mentioned it again. They were back to their teasing relationship that had its tender moments. Samuel seemed to realize that Julie was Dylan's girl and had shied away, seldom entering the house when he and Julie's father returned from the field.

Julie picked up her pace. In the distance the snow-covered peaks were cloud shrouded, but here below it was a white fairyland with dazzling icicles hanging from the rooftops. Hitting a branch overhead, she knocked down a flurry of snow over her wool knit cap, then exulted in the snowflakes and brisk day. Julie sensed this was a precious time of her life, a time to be treasured.

Arriving home, Julie poked up the fire

before removing her jacket and hat, threw on several logs, and lit the well-trimmed oil lamps that gave the room a warm glow. She missed her mother, not only for her love, but for the care she gave to keeping house. With a pang Julie wondered how Granny Ruth was faring.

After the fire was roaring and the beef and cabbage were simmering, she hurried out to the shed to feed Cinder. Using a pitchfork, she tossed fodder to her small mare, who danced and snorted. "Hello, old girl," Julie said, her breath forming frosty puffs.

She patted Cinder's neck, and the mare responded by tossing her glossy mane and nickering in pleasure at her mistress's touch. Julie could feel how thick Cinder's winter coat had grown. "Another two months, Cinder," she promised, yearning to go for a ride, "and we'll be back on the mountain trail." She nestled her head into Cinder's mane.

"Hey! What does an Irish Terrier have to do to earn the affection you give Cinder?" Dylan asked laughingly, as he stood outlined in the doorway. His plaid scarf dangled jauntily across his coat and snowflakes sparkled in his jet-black hair.

"You have to be a horse," she replied mischievously, conscious of the crisp, fresh scent Dylan exuded.

Dylan whinnied playfully, moving to Julie's side. "Is it good enough if I'm a horse *lover*?"

"Hmmm," she countered. "That's close." She smiled at Dylan. "I thought you loved only *iron* horses, not *real* horses."

"Ahhh, there's where you're wrong, me darling. As much as I love trains, I love horses, too. Didn't you know Ireland is called the 'Land of the Horse'? And that someday I'll be rich enough to buy you a sure-footed Connemara pony from Ireland. They're the best horse jumpers anywhere."

"I wouldn't trade Cinder for all the Connemaras in the world!" she stated firmly, brushing Cinder's mane to a black sheen.

"That's what's grand about you, Julie. You're loyal!" Nonchalantly he picked up a brush and helped curry Cinder. "Will you always be this loyal — even to your first love?"

"My first love?" she echoed, raising her brows. "And who might *that* be?"

Dylan brushed faster. "Well, sure, and I don't know if you don't, but I'll wager it's not someone called Samuel Harper."

"Did I hear my name mentioned?" came a voice from behind.

Julie spun about. There stood Samuel and Julie's father. Blood rushed to her face, and she didn't know what to reply.

Jay Fulton, to cover his daughter's obvious embarrassment, came up to Cinder, feeding the little mare an apple. He gave

Julie a sidelong glance and said casually, "I hope you don't mind, dear, but I've asked Sam to stay for supper. We still haven't finished our map work."

Dylan whistled, brushing Cinder's hindquarters. He glanced over the mare's back at Julie, winking.

Flustered, she looked away from Dylan's amused smile and into Samuel's solemn face. "Of-of course," she stammered, her cheeks still tingling. "I'd love you to stay, Samuel."

Dylan's tune became louder and merrier, as if he was looking forward to spending an evening being compared with Samuel.

When Michael came home, Julie set an additional plate while the men discussed the railroad's progress and the bad weather. She smiled to herself when she heard Dylan say in his lilting brogue, "The snow is enough to knock the top off your head."

"It sure is," Samuel agreed. "But I admire the Gandy Dancers that keep pushing ahead in this snow and ice."

Even Samuel was using railroad expressions, thought Julie. Gandy Dancer, an Irish jig, was another nickname given to the Irish workers. She was pleased that Samuel and Dylan seemed to be getting along so well.

When Julie set the great steaming platter of beef and cabbage on the table, the hungry men sat down without being called. Using a wooden paddle, she removed hot soda bread from the oven, then sat down herself.

"Well, Mr. Fulton," Dylan asked, dishing up a generous helping of the stew, "have you and Samuel figured out a way around Echo Canyon?"

Jay Fulton, accepting the platter, said, "We'll have to blast a tunnel through the mountain."

"Glory be!" Dylan exclaimed. "Another mountain tunnel! That's the third one since we left Cheyenne. That will set us back a good two weeks!"

"Better a tunnel than switchbacks or laying track around the mountain like a coiled snake," Samuel said quietly.

Dylan glanced at Samuel, nodding slowly, respecting his judgment. "I suppose you're right."

"Of course he is," Jay Fulton said, making a steeple of his fingers. "All we're waiting for now is the next train carrying the explosives." He shook his head. "If it *ever* gets through! When I came in, the clouds were dark, and the wind was picking up. We're in for another snowstorm."

"Too bad we didn't learn from the Central Pacific," Michael said, "and build snowsheds. I read in the paper that Mr. Crocker bragged that none of the Central Pacific trains ran more than two hours late — even in the worst blizzard."

As if to punctuate his last word, the wind tore a shutter loose, banging it against the window.

"I'd better fasten that shutter," muttered Mr. Fulton. He looked at his assistant. "Sam, you and I had better postpone our work until tomorrow. That is, if we can get out of our front doors in the morning. You'd better head for home while you can still get there!"

"You're right, Mr. Fulton," Samuel said, hurriedly eating the last bite of his baked apple. "My uncle will be worried." He glanced at Julie. "That was a wonderful dinner," he said appreciatively, rising to his feet. "A typically Irish meal, wasn't it?"

Dylan in one fluid motion, stood, too, grinning broadly. "As typically Irish as the name O'Kelly."

Samuel faced Dylan, smiling. "Doesn't the 'O' in your name mean 'the son of'?"

"That's close, me lad," Dylan said admiringly. "But the 'O' stands for 'the grandson of.' If my name started with 'Mc' like Old Tom McNamara, then it would mean the 'son of.'" He clapped Samuel on the back. "But you're learning! Don't worry, Sam, me boy. I'll set you straight on Irish names and history — on *everything* Irish!"

"That would be fascinating," replied

Samuel, pulling his felt cap down to his soft brown eyes.

Julie shot him a quick look. Was Sam being sarcastic? Maybe not, she thought, for Samuel's smiling eyes shone with genuine interest.

"Good!" Dylan said, tossing his cap in the air and deftly catching it behind him. "Here's a riddle to start your first lesson:

It's round as an apple,
As deep as a cup,
And all the men in Ireland
Could not lift it up!"

Samuel chuckled as he put on his mittens. "A well!"

Dylan's blue eyes widened. "How did you know that?"

"I've been around you Gandy Dancers long enough to pick up a few things."

"Samuel, we're going to get along just fine," Dylan said, as he lifted his sheepskin from the coat rack and shrugged his shoulders into it. "On the way home I'll tell you the story of the Irishman and the leprechaun." He turned to Julie. "I'd love to stay, but that howling wind means I'd better get home, too. But that was a dinner I'll cherish. Just for me, wasn't it?"

She nodded mutely, not daring to look at Samuel.

Samuel, however, was listening to her father as he set up a new appointment for their work. If Samuel had heard Dylan, he didn't seem to mind.

Dylan tilted his green wool cap over one ear. "Come on, Samuel. Let's go."

When the door opened, snow blew across the room and the oil lamp flickered, almost going out.

After the door shut behind them, Michael helped her clear the table. "Julie, your two suitors are quite friendly. You should be pleased!"

"Oh, I am," she assured him, scraping the dishes. She wasn't sure they were both *suitors*, but she knew they were definitely her friends. And she knew that in a frontier town like Crooked Branch, the more friends you had, the better your chances of survival.

Chapter Seven

JULIE hurried home from the depot, clutching the two letters. Letters from Mother. She rushed in, and even before removing her coat and scarf, she heated the coffee. Next, she propped up the letters against the dried flower and herb arrangement on the table. One was addressed to her father, the other to Michael and her. She couldn't wait to read the contents of the thick envelope, but she intended to savor every word.

When the coffee came to a boil, she poured a cup, seated herself at the kitchen table, slit open the flap, and began to read:

December 31, 1868

Dearest Julie and Michael,

Granny Ruth is still very ill, but today she sat up for the first time, drank a cup of beef broth, and had a spoonful of custard. It breaks my heart to see her so thin, but hopefully she's on the road to recovery.

Michael, I accompanied Liza and her mother to the Opera House last week. Liza said she mailed you a long letter. Perhaps you have it by now. Your fiancée looks as vibrant as ever, working every day at the assayer's office. Although the gold rush is over and fewer miners come in to have their claims registered, she's still very busy weighing ore.

Julie had to smile when she remembered how yesterday Michael had carefully folded Liza's letter and squirreled it away to his room. It was obvious he didn't intend to share Liza's words with anyone else. He was really in love!

Bowing her head, she continued reading:

I've been cleaning this big house and cooking. The one bright spot in my day is the late afternoon. While Granny Ruth naps, I take a long walk, usually across the bridge over the South Platte River to the Old Mill. This winter is quite mild in Denver, and I love the frosty air, especially after being in a darkened sick room all day.

I miss my telegrapher post, but I know you're doing a good job, Julie. By the way, I met your best friend, Agatha, at the milliner's shop yesterday. She looks elegant and radiantly happy. She's just become engaged to Henry Ramsey. They plan to marry in June. She promised to write to you, dear, but wishes you'd write, too. Why don't you do that?

I hear Crooked Branch is snowbound, and the Union Pacific is having problems getting trains through. Aren't those new rotary plows able to clear the tracks?

You should see how Denver has changed! It's a new city! Completely rebuilt after the devastating fire we had. Remember how close it came to our house?

Julie closed her eyes. How could she ever forget that terrifying day five years ago? She had been ten years old and had been sent to the cobbler's. As she had neared Main Street, the sky turned crimson, and it seemed the whole town was ablaze. Several burning buildings had collapsed near her! Panic-stricken, she had raced home, praying her family was alive. The smoke had scorched her eyes, making them stream with tears, but she didn't care as she rushed into the house. Panting from terror and fear, she had rushed first into her mother's arms, then her father's, and then Michael's. And, last but not least, she had hugged their bulldog, Tuffy. What happiness she'd felt that day!

But Denver was a long time recovering, for a second disaster had happened the following year. A lump came to her throat at the memory of the flash flood that had engulfed the city, sweeping away the city hall built on stilts. Poor Tuffy. He had almost drowned. He had clambered to safety on a large timber. She could still see herself crying on the riverbank when her bulldog floated swiftly downstream.

Then, heedless of her safety, she had recklessly plunged into the swollen waters of Cherry Creek. She'd been determined to rescue Tuffy! The debris-filled waters, brackish and swollen, had closed over her head. Michael, with a superhuman effort, had furiously jerked her back onto the riverbank. Then, without a moment's hesitation he had dived in, swam out, and grasped Tuffy by the collar. When her exhausted brother had fought his way back to shore, she'd clung to him and let Tuffy lick away her tears. Sweet dog! How she missed him, but he had died of old age just before they moved to Crooked Branch. Her father had offered to buy her another puppy, but she hadn't been ready at the time. No dog could take the place of Tuffy. Perhaps now, though, she should think of getting another dog. Maybe the hurt of losing Tuffy had blurred enough that she'd be able to love a new puppy.

But her thoughts were wandering, she realized, as she turned the letter's second page:

How did you celebrate New Year's Eve? By the time you receive this it will be 1869! Hard to believe!

Tonight is New Year's Eve, but it's just another quiet evening at home to me. I plan to read aloud to Mother. I'm reading a new novel by Emily Brontë called *Wuthering Heights*. We're both enjoying it.

Well, my dears, it's time to draw this letter to a close. I wish I could be with you, but it looks as though I'll be here at least six more weeks.

Take care of each other, my Julie and Michael. I love you.

A kiss,
Mother

Think of it, Julie sighed. Agatha, at sixteen, would soon marry. She must write and congratulate her. Maybe they'd return to Denver in June in time for her wedding. A pang struck her heart. But she didn't really *want* to leave this railroad town or Dylan or Samuel. Besides, things wouldn't be the same between her and Agatha. And in two months Julie would be sixteen, too — old enough to marry Dylan, as he had so quickly pointed out not too long ago.

Eighteen sixty-nine! A new year and a new beginning, Julie mused, pouring more coffee and leaning back in her chair. What would it bring? How different her New Year's Eve had been from Mother's. She had made a special dinner for the family, which now seemed to include Dylan and Samuel.

Later, while Michael fiddled, Dylan had taught everyone an Irish jig. It was marvelous to see how well Dylan and Samuel got along. It was evident their friendship was strong and secure. Although Sam no longer made romantic overtures, still she had caught him staring at her with his soft eyes. She wondered if Dylan had noticed. She grinned at the prospect of Dylan's being jealous. He had too much self-confidence to be bothered by any attention Samuel paid her. She caught her breath as she remembered Dylan's lips brushing against her hair. A warm glow touched her heart. She was in love with Dylan, there was no mistake about that!

Suddenly the door was flung wide, letting in an icy blast.

"Julie!" Michael shouted, his worried face red from the cold. "Come, quick! There's been an accident on the "Z"! Father and Samuel were on the train!"

At first his words didn't register.

"Julie! Come on!" he said impatiently. "The train was carrying nitroglycerine!"

Her stomach clenched tight. Father and Sam might be dead! She set her cup down so hard the hot coffee splashed onto her wrist. Unheedful of the scalding liquid, she grabbed her jacket, dashing outdoors with Michael.

The dreaded "Z"! How often she'd heard her father advise Jack Casement not to build this eight-mile zigzag track over the ice and snow. But the Casement brothers couldn't wait for the spring thaws. They needed to push forward to beat the Central Pacific, no matter what the cost. And this winter was not going to hold them back!

Over the engineers' protests the "Z" track had been built without any ballast or grading to steady it. Dylan, part of the iron crews at the head of Echo Canyon, had labored by lantern light, scratching a narrow path in the hard red rock of the canyon and building rickety stiltwork to form the perilous "Z". Supply trains were getting through and the materials could go forward to the diggers in the west end. The cars, though, now traveled slowly over the plunging "Z" curve, and the crews were poised to jump at the least hint of derailment. The Casements risked workers' lives, but she knew they risked their own, as well. There wasn't a day they didn't labor right along with their men.

The Casements had been in trouble before because of the number of railroad men that had been maimed or killed. Yet, she thought, her chest so tight she was afraid it would burst, if the Casements had sacrificed Samuel's and Father's lives for their railroad, she'd personally travel to Washington, D.C., to testify against them. This time they wouldn't get off so easily!

Her mind reeled with confusion. How could she think of all this when Father and Samuel might be lying in the snow? If the nitroglycerine had exploded, what chance did they have?

She glanced at Michael, whose fiery red hair blew about his rugged face. She took a running step to keep up with him. "Michael," she asked fearfully, hardly daring to breathe, "do you think they're all right?"

Michael burrowed his head deeper into his jacket collar against the wind. "I don't know," he mumbled. "I only heard that the train had slid into the canyon." He stopped and confronted her, his gray eyes dark with pain. "You must be brave, Julie. We don't know what we'll find at the bottom of that canyon."

She averted her face, fighting back tears. No, no, she groaned inwardly, at the same time praying silently, "Let them be all right!" Enough men had died for the Union Pacific, and even more had been killed on the Central

Chapter
Eight

SHOUTS and laughter filled the crisp air of the canyon. Were her ears playing tricks on her? Julie wondered. Who could be laughing? What was going on?

Rounding the bend, Julie saw the mangled train. The twisted wreck was plunged into a gigantic snowdrift. One derailed car teetered perilously on the edge of a deep drop-off. A few men were dazed, but others were joking as they walked about in circles, amazed at their good fortune — they were alive! The snow, cushioning their fall, had saved everyone, including the engineer and fireman.

When Jay Fulton glimpsed Michael and Julie, he waved exuberantly. "Over here!" he yelled.

Amazed, but with a soaring, glad feeling,

she grabbed Michael's hand and raced down the incline to where her father and the rest of the men were pounding each other on the back, shaking hands, laughing, and brushing off their snow-covered coats. Although they were all safe, iron rails were strewn about the snow. Julie closed her eyes with relief. The unpredictable nitroglycerine had not exploded!

Hiram Harper, standing beside his hurt nephew, helped Samuel staunch a flow of blood from his temple. Julie wanted to go to Samuel, but first she had to see if her father was really unhurt.

"Father!" she called, "are you all right?"

"I couldn't be better, dear." A smile crossed his face and his gray eyes twinkled. "Except for my mussed hair and being buried in a snow mound, I'm very much all right!" Enthusiastically, he caught his daughter up in his arms and swung her around. "In fact, I'm a very lucky man! We've been cursing the snow all winter, but without it, I wouldn't be standing here now." He set her down and kissed her nose. "Julie, your flaming red hair and freckles never looked more beautiful."

"You look pretty beautiful yourself," she teased. And he did, too, in his checked trousers and knee-length overcoat. His smooth, round face didn't have a mark on it!

Michael came up, hugging his father. "It's

great to see you alive, Father. Julie and I didn't know what to expect when we rounded that curve!"

Grinning, Julie stood on tiptoe and kissed her father's cheeks. "Father," she said, "I'd better see how seriously Samuel is hurt."

"Yes, run along, Julie. I'll see you at suppertime." He faced Michael, explaining with vivid hand motions how the train slid into the canyon.

Hiram Harper, arguing with Jack Casement over the train wreck, put up his hand as if to stop Julie, but she hurried by him to reach Samuel.

"Samuel!" she said with concern. "You had a close call." Gently, she examined his deep cut.

"It isn't much," he explained with a shrug, but he seemed to enjoy her attention. "When the train took its plunge, I was thrown against the window, smashing it." He smiled ruefully. "It could have been worse." He paused, his brown eyes fastened on hers. "I haven't had a chance to say this, Julie, but I've missed you!"

"But we've been together a lot," Julie protested. "Your work with Father brings you to our house often."

"That's what I mean. There's always someone around." He gave her a shy smile. "I wish it were picnic weather again. Those were some of the best times I've ever had." He tore his eyes away and gazed at the sheets of ice hanging from the canyon walls and the deep snow. "But it will be a long time before we'll see the flowers."

"And the Indians," she teased, grinning.

"And the Indians," he repeated solemnly. "What a surprise you were that day, Julie!"

"An unpleasant surprise, I'm sure," she answered playfully.

"No, I wouldn't say that," he said slowly, his gentle brown eyes brightening, "but I must admit I like it better when you're acting like a lady than when you're shooting at Indians!"

A brief frown flitted across her face. Then she smiled impishly and looked directly at him. "Really, Samuel, even wounded as you are, you're still concerned about the way I act."

He caught and held her hand. "Julie," he whispered, "don't tease me." Her smile faded as he continued. "I know you're spoken for by my good friend, and you couldn't do better than Dylan," he paused, "but if you ever need me, I'll always be here for you." He bent close.

How sweet and caring Samuel was, Julie thought. Breathlessly, as his lips softly brushed her cheek, she waited for his kiss. "Julie," Samuel murmured, but Hiram Harper interrupted him.

"Well, Nephew!" boomed his uncle, approaching suddenly. "Let's go home!" He turned his head. "I've invited your father to the house, Julie. Won't you join us?"

She had the uncomfortable feeling that Hiram Harper was hoping she'd refuse, but she responded quickly, "Yes, I'd like to."

"I invited Michael, too, but the wreck needs to be cleared. He's part of the clean-up crew." Hiram's eyes glittered contemptuously. "Jack Casement doesn't waste a minute!" He shook his head vehemently. "A stop order for work on the railroad doesn't bother him. He's going against direct orders from Washington, D.C.!"

Startled, Julie glanced at Hiram's angry, contorted face. He chuckled harshly when he caught her wide eyes on him. "I'll explain later, Julie," he said smoothly, recovering his composure. "Right now we need to get my wounded nephew home."

Samuel, with a sheepish smile, gave Julie a sidelong look as if to say how sorry he was that his uncle had interrupted his kiss.

Hiram, Samuel, Jay, and Julie rode in a splendid coach pulled by two superb horses. Julie touched the plush velvet interior, admiring the rich crimson fabric. The two small lanterns in the front and the black lacquer trim were extravagant appointments. Well, she thought, why *shouldn't* Mr. Harper have a luxurious coach? After all, he was the owner of a whole stagecoach line!

Pulling into the circular drive of Hiram Harper's large white house, Julie noticed the gingerbread carvings about the porch. Another carriage had just arrived, and the driver, a striking woman, dressed in a white fur-trimmed coat with a matching toque hat and muff, waved. "Hello, Hiram, dear. Where have you been?" Her vivid lips parted in a broad smile, and her eyes, outlined with black charcoal, crinkled.

Coming closer, Julie could see the woman was older than she'd first thought — about her mother's age, she judged. All at once she recognized Nell Brannigan, the owner of the Red Bull Saloon.

"Hello, Nell," Hiram greeted her grudgingly. He jumped out of the coach. "Look, I'm busy now. I have a meeting." He didn't bother to introduce her. "You run along back to town. I'll see you later tonight." He wheeled about, helping Julie down.

Nell, her underlip jutting forth, said, "And I rode all the way out here just to see you."

Hiram's eyes narrowed to a slate-blue and he whirled about. "I said, I'd see you *later*, Nell," he retorted firmly. "Now, good-bye."

"Men," Nell muttered scathingly, giving Julie a knowing look beneath raised, penciled brows. With a resigned shrug, she cracked a whip over her horse's rump and sailed down the drive.

In the parlor Hiram jovially poured three glasses of whiskey from a crystal decanter. Serving Samuel first, he ordered, "Drink this, my boy. It'll help clear your head."

Reluctantly, Sam took the glass. "Thanks, Uncle Hiram," he said.

"Drink up!" Hiram commanded.

Samuel, after an instant's hesitation, gulped down the whiskey. He treated it as if it were medicine, and the sooner taken, the sooner it was over with.

Julie suppressed a pained smile when Samuel sputtered and coughed. He wasn't like some of the workers, who seemed to thrive on the fiery stuff. Julie pitied Samuel, who seemed to be drinking the whiskey only to please his uncle.

Hiram laughed, slapping Sam on the back. He glanced at Julie. "And what will you have my dear, a glass of milk?" His laugh erupted into a guffaw.

A hot flush stained her cheeks. "No, thank you."

"Now, Jay," Hiram said, dismissing Julie as if she were a pesky mosquito, "I wanted to talk to you about the Indians piling iron rails on the track about twenty miles south of here."

Julie's father stared, complete surprise on his face. "I thought the Casement brothers had signed an agreement with the Cheyenne. Jack has even given them free passes to ride on the train!"

"My driver saw them," Hiram said quietly, fingering his pointed beard. "The Cheyenne are up to no good, doing everything possible to impede the railroad's progress." He put a booted foot on a velvet hassock. "Not that I care, but the Casements are asking for trouble, and if they're not careful, we'll have an Indian war on our hands!"

He hit his fist into his palm. "The Casements dare to go against the President's order! The money's run out, yet those two go right on building as fast as they can. They're defying Washington because they know how slowly the government acts!"

He stalked over to the fireplace, pounding the mantelpiece. "Jack Casement's going to be stopped if I have to do it myself!"

He confronted Julie. "Tomorrow I want you to send a telegraph message to Andrew Johnson. He might be a lame duck, but he's still our President! The Casements, of course, think they can get around Johnson by dealing directly with Ulysses S. Grant. They know Grant will be sworn in as President at the March inauguration ceremony. Well, Grant and his former Union generals, Sheridan and Sherman, might be big supporters of the Union Pacific, but," he snorted derisively,

"I'm going to nip their little game in the bud!"

Settling his bulk in the swivel chair before a large rolltop desk, Hiram dipped the quill-tip pen into the ink well. After a moment's thought he began to write, the plumed pen furiously wagging back and forth.

When finished, he pushed back his chair and chuckled, admiring his handiwork. "This should stop the Casement boys!" Clearing his throat he read:

TO PRESIDENT ANDREW JOHNSON:
CASEMENT BROTHERS PROCEEDING WITH
LAYING TRACK. SEND SOLDIERS.
      HIRAM HARPER
        CROOKED BRANCH, UTAH

"Well," Hiram snapped, looking defiantly at Jay Fulton and Samuel, "don't look so down in the mouth. I'm only obeying the law that President Johnson set down!"

Jay Fulton ran his fingers through his thick hair. "There's no need to send that, Hiram. I realize you have a legitimate gripe with the railroad, but by the time Andrew Johnson does anything, Grant will be our new President. Besides," he said with a frown, "Johnson has gone through one impeachment trial, and I don't think he'll needlessly stick his neck out again."

Hiram, disregarding his words, faced Julie, smiling. "Send this out first thing in the morning, Julie."

Julie, feeling as if ice water had been spilled down her spine, reluctantly took the paper. To think she had to be the one to betray the people she loved! Folding the message with trembling fingers, she tucked it into her pocket, wondering if she'd be able to forget Hiram's supercilious smile.

In dismay, she glanced first at Samuel, then her father. She believed as fervently in the railroad as they did. But being a trusted telegraph operator, she had to send Hiram's message, a message that would shatter almost more dreams than she could count.

Chapter Nine

IT was too bad the downed telegraph wires had been repaired after the last big snow, Julie thought regretfully as she transmitted Hiram's telegraph message. Could President Johnson *really* halt the railroad construction? But when she remembered Michael's words, she was cheered a bit. He had told her not to worry — that Dan and Jack Casement would do whatever they pleased, and it pleased them to push on to Ogden. No restraining order was going to stop them! Then, too, the rich men who had invested in the Union Pacific wouldn't allow the railroad to go bankrupt. And a way would be found to keep supplies coming in and to subsidize the payroll — at least until March, when Grant became President.

Julie wanted to forget the message she had just sent. She decided to study the Morse code — not that she didn't know it perfectly, but she liked to practice. Shutting off the telegraph key so it wouldn't transmit, she clicked out one fake message after another. Her adept, slender fingers didn't make a mistake. She tapped out the sentence THE CAT ATE THE RAT to test her skill.

What an insignificant sentence, she thought as she tapped out a more meaningful one — JULIE LOVES DYLAN.

She smiled at the sentiment and was pleased at her accuracy. But she knew she mustn't keep the machine off too long.

It was fortunate she turned it back on when she did because a real message soon crackled over the wires. Quickly transposing the dots and dashes into words, she hastily scribbled:

INDIANS DERAIL SUPPLY TRAIN TEN MILES WEST OF BITTER CREEK. ENGINEER AND FIREMAN KILLED. SEND HELP.

Julie stared at the words. Hiram Harper was right! This could be the start of an Indian war. For months the Indians had been peaceful. In fact, there had been peace ever since they had pow-wowed with the Casements. But something must have gone wrong. Didn't the Indians know they couldn't stop the railroad?

The painful memory of an Indian attack nine months before, shortly after their arrival from Denver, came flooding back. The Cheyenne had tried to stop the train by lying in ambush. When the train whistle had blown, six horsemen on either side of the track had pulled a wire taut in the path of the oncoming engine. Once and for all the Indians would capture the Iron Horse — or so they had thought. The engine, however, had plowed through the stretched wire as if it had been a mere piece of silk, sweeping the two lead Indians off their horses under the locomotive's wheels and scattering the others. Five Indians had been killed that day, all in the name of the railroad.

Since that time the Cheyenne and Sioux hadn't tried to stop a single train. Thanks to a few bitter lessons and the agreement with Jack Casement!

But now the Cheyenne were trying to stop the train by other means. Why? Oh, please, she prayed, don't let a war erupt between the railroad men and the Indians. There could be only one winner — the railroad. But the delay and cost in lives would be intolerable, as well as an irreparable blot on the building of the transcontinental railroad.

Shaking free her dismal thoughts, Julie

hurriedly put on her coat and rushed out to find Jack Casement.

She found the construction boss in the tunnel of Echo Canyon. Along with his workers, he was wielding a pick-axe. He was dressed like them, too, in knee-top boots, a lumberjack jacket, and fur hat.

"What is it?" he rapped out, continuing to slog away at the hard rock. His profile had an inherent strength to it as he bent over his task.

"Train Number Nineteen has been derailed by Indians," she burst out, her words tumbling over one another. "The engineer and firemen were killed. They need help right away!"

He spun his short muscular body and yelled, "Dylan O'Kelly! Get over here!"

Dylan threw down his sledgehammer, moving quickly to Jack Casement's side. When Dylan saw Julie, his dazzling blue eyes danced, easing the lines in his tired face. "Julie," he said, astonished. "What are you doing here?"

"Julie Fulton's here with bad news," Jack broke in. "I want you to take ten men, Dylan, and head up a rescue crew. There's been a train wreck this side of Bitter Creek. Sean Callahan and Tom Riley were killed." Jack pressed his lips together, leaning on his axe handle. "We don't know how many others are still trapped in the wreckage."

Dylan's stricken expression spoke volumes. "What next?" he asked in despair.

"I still can't believe the Indians would do such a thing," Julie protested weakly, hating to believe what she knew to be true.

"Believe it!" Dylan snapped, his jaw tightening. "Two men are dead. What more proof do you need?" Abruptly he wheeled about and strode over to his crew. "Jim, Clancy, Pat, Frank! Come with me! We've got some dirty business to attend to. We'll pick up more men at camp." He walked back to Julie. "I'll see you tomorrow if all goes well." His eyes softened and he squeezed her hand. "Sorry if I yelled at you, me darling. It's just that this is such back-breaking work — and then to have *this* happen!" He bowed his head, rubbing his forehead. "Sean," he murmured, "was a friend of mine."

"Oh, Dylan, I'm so sorry," she said softly, sympathy filling her heart.

Their eyes locked while he touched her cheek. "I need you, Julie. Don't ever leave me and my wicked temper."

She smiled, blinking back tears. "Never, Dylan. I'm afraid you're stuck with me."

A small smile flitted across his strong features before he pulled himself away. Facing his men, he ordered crisply, "Follow me!"

Miserably, Julie watched them trudge through the snow. She knew that digging hurt men out of a twisted wreck would be a grim, difficult job, especially in this icy cold. Hurrying back toward the telegraph office, she planned to send a message to Bitter Creek. They'd be relieved to hear that help was on the way.

On a track siding she stopped at a bonfire where Michael, along with several other workers, were warming themselves.

"Hi, Julie!" several of them greeted her.

"How's our cheerful telegraph operator?" another asked.

"Not too well," she said. "You heard about the wreck at Bitter Creek."

"We did!" Michael said, his cheeks flaming in anger. "It's time the Cheyenne were taught a lesson!"

It saddened Julie to hear them talk this way. It could only mean trouble. Dead men on both sides.

Michael, always sensitive to her feelings, pointed to the leaping flames to change the subject. "How do you like our one hundred dollar fire, Julie?" he asked with a smile.

She stared at him blankly, his words not registering. "What do you mean, Michael?"

"We can't chop any trees because of the snow, so we've got to burn rail ties. Each one is worth two dollars a piece." He half turned to a chunky fellow beside him. "We've piled fifty on the fire, right, John?"

The black-bearded man bobbed his head, grinning. "Let's go back to the digging, fellows," he said. " 'Bye Julie. And remember, we depend on you!" Giving her a thumbs up sign, they left.

Briefly Julie held out her hands above the flames and let the warmth engulf her. A one hundred dollar fire, she thought in awe. Was it any wonder the railroad was nearly out of money?

"Oh, Michael," she said, a catch in her throat. "Everything is so awful — the train wreck with men killed, the stop work order, the Indians. Where's it going to end?"

Michael stared at the fire. His mouth became a stubborn, downward line. "I don't know, Julie. We're so close to meeting the Central Pacific. Why, just this morning we nailed up a sign on a lone pine tree atop Blue Summit. The words stand out sharp and clear! 1000 MILES WEST OF OMAHA." He inhaled deeply. "We're near, but sometimes it doesn't look as if we'll meet those Central Pacific workers after all."

"Michael, everything we've hoped for," she said with a catch in her voice, gazing about, "is going to stop in this desolate little town." A shiver went through her.

"Not necessarily," Michael said, staring down at his little sister. He brightened, patting her cheek. "Remember, Julie, we don't have red hair for nothing!" A muscle moved in his square face. "We'll fight every inch of the way. I don't care if it's snow, Indians, or no pay. And with leaders like Dan and Jack we're bound to win!"

"You've cheered me up," she said, smiling. "But then, you always do." She knew he was right, too. With fighters like Father, Mother, Michael, and Dylan — and yes, herself — how could they lose? "And now, Michael dear," she said lightly, "I've got to send a message to Bitter Creek."

"And I'd better get back to spiking rails!" He started away, then stopped in midstride, turning. "I'll be working the late shift, so don't wait up for me." With a wave he headed back to the tunnel.

On the way back to the office she couldn't help thinking of Michael's friend and his words, "We depend on you, Julie." How sweet that sounded. If she could be like her mother, things couldn't be *all* bad.

When she returned to the depot, she sent the message, then straightened the office. By noon her shift was over and she hurried home. She wouldn't see Dylan tonight, perhaps not for several days. Samuel and Father had gone up ahead to Weber Canyon to do additional surveying, and her brother was working late. For once she had the whole house to herself. It was a strange feeling, for seldom was she alone. Tonight, however, with the wind howling and with more snow falling, she reveled in the cozy house. After reading a few chapters in a mystery book that one of the men had left at the telegraph office, she went up to bed.

Undressing down to her lace camisole and pantaloons, she stood before the full-length mirror. The lacy straps and bodice showed off her slender shoulders and graceful neck.

Brushing out her long, abundant hair, glowing bright auburn in the lamplight, she studied her reflection. She had changed from the freckle-faced girl of Denver days. Her round cheeks had disappeared, giving way to hollow planes in an oval face. Play-acting, she fluttered her thick long eyelashes and wet her lips. Her green eyes were still wide-apart but seemed larger and a deeper jade. Even her body, which had been wiry, was taking on new contours. Although she could still span her slim waist with her two hands, her whole body was more rounded, yet slimmer, if that was possible.

Placing her hands on her hips, she moved, swaying toward the mirror. Most of her freckles seemed to fade into the deep gold of her satin-smooth skin. Her wide genial mouth curved into a secret smile as she thought of Dylan.

All at once the smile she was trying to make look coy and inviting gave way to a grin of amusement. Who did she think she was, prancing about and trying to act like a glamour girl? Dylan would love it! Samuel would hate it! Or would he?

Wriggling her flannel nightgown over her head, Julie pulled it down, made a funny face at the mirror, then blew out the lamp's flame. Slipping beneath the flannel sheets and down quilt, she snuggled beneath the warm layers. The frosty moon illuminated the night and bathed her room in a silver glow. The ice-laden tree branches glistened like crystal fairy wands. How winter could change the landscape, just as Crooked Branch, for all its wildness, had changed her. It wasn't only her body that had visibly changed. It was something inside her, too. Something no one could see and only *she* could understand.

In the last few months she'd become a woman — no, not quite a woman, but she had grown up. She was a more self-assured, a more thinking and a more caring person. Was it her new responsibilities as a telegraph operator? Was it Dylan? Samuel? She tossed in bed, pulling the covers up to her chin. How could she know *what* it was!

A stab of apprehension swept over her. Did she really want to grow up and leave behind that little girl that loved to ride and shoot? How could she give up the things she loved the most? Was that what her new maturity meant? Then she'd be switched if she wanted to become a woman. On the other hand, be-

coming a woman meant more freedom —
not asking permission to do this or that, for
instance — but it also meant more responsibilities.

She pummeled her pillow. She didn't know
if she liked these new feelings stirring within
her. Perhaps she shouldn't go back to Denver,
but follow Dylan and move from one railroad
town to another. For some girls, like Agatha,
such a prospect would be too bleak to contem-
plate. But for Julie, the prospect was a thrilling one!

Chapter Ten

THE next day Julie sent a telegraph message for Number Thirty-three locomotive to pull over on a siding and make way for supply train Number Six to go ahead. She had just finished when a message from her mother clicked over the wires:

GRANNY RUTH MUCH IMPROVED.
WILL COME HOME SOON.

Julie was elated. Granny was better! What wonderful news! How she had missed her mother! If only her father weren't out in the field so she could run and tell him the good news.

Poking up the fire in the potbellied stove, she glanced about the small office that she'd become so familiar with these past months. A rough-hewn bench in the corner and her desk and chair were all the furnishings in the depot. She smiled. *Her* desk and chair? Not much longer. Mother would be here before long and reclaim her job. Eager as Julie was to see her mother, she still felt a twinge of remorse in having to give up her telegraph post.

A figure went by the window, followed shortly by the door opening.

"Hello, Julie."

"Dylan!" she said, rising and going to him. She was dismayed at his appearance. His forehead was creased, and taut lines hovered about his generous mouth. "Oh, Dylan," she said tenderly. "I'm glad you're back. Was the rescue a difficult one?"

"There will be a double funeral tomorrow for Sean and Tom," he said grimly. "The train was a twisted mass of iron. We managed to clean it up with Locomotive Number Nine." He sank down on the bench, sprawling his long legs in front of him. His boots were caked with snow and mud. "About six feet of track had been yanked up, sending the train down into a ravine. Horses will haul supplies until repairs can be made."

"The Cheyenne are really out to stop the railroad, aren't they?" she stated quietly.

"That they are! The brakeman riding the caboose caught sight of the Indian leader.

He wore an elaborate purple-and-white feathered headdress."

"Hmmm," she mused. "The same chieftain I saw at Stony Point."

"Well, he won't be around much longer!" Dylan vowed.

"Oh?" she said, waiting expectantly for an explanation.

"Jack Casement has issued Winchester rifles to all the workers. From now on, we don't work unless our guns are with us." He paused. "And if we see any Indians lurking around, we're supposed to shoot first and ask questions afterwards!"

A knot of fear twisted her stomach. "Couldn't this be solved without any killing? Another powwow, perhaps?"

"Always the optimistic one, aren't you, me darling? No, I'm afraid it's gone too far this time. Now we fight!" He rose. "But right now I don't want to do any fighting — not even thinking about it." He yawned and stretched. "All I want is a ten-hour sleep."

He pulled her to him, kissing her lightly on the forehead. "You're my special girl," he said, brushing her hair with his lips. "I'll come by tomorrow." He gave her a slow grin. "If you have no objections."

"None whatsoever," she replied pertly, giving him a bright smile in return.

With his old, carefree bravado, Dylan blew her a kiss and left.

Turning back to the telegraph machine, Julie smiled, almost hugging herself. Tomorrow she'd see Dylan. What a delightful prospect!

But the next day Crooked Branch was caught up in a blinding blizzard, and in the next few weeks she saw very little of Dylan. Telegraph poles were blown down, and she found it almost impossible to get the front door open. Drifts were as deep as twenty-five feet in the cuts, and mail service from Omaha was completely blocked. Over two hundred westbound passengers were stranded at Laramie.

After the big storm, the tracks were replaced at Bitter Creek, and Julie was kept busy sending messages to the backed up supply trains that now came pouring in. Then, too, it was reported that the Central Pacific was moving forward at a rapid rate. The Casement brothers, not to be outdone, pushed their men feverishly and the rails crept forward as the winter's snow and ice began to melt.

On March tenth, her sixteenth birthday, Julie went for a walk, kicking at the sludge heaps with her boots. No one had remembered her special day. Not a soul, she thought disconsolately, had even said "Happy Birthday."

Entering the house, she wearily took off

her hat and coat. She knew if she were really grown-up, her forgotten birthday wouldn't matter so much.

"Hello, darling! Happy Birthday!" There stood her father holding a large package tied with a gold bow. He smiled smugly, as if pleased with himself for buying something she would like.

"You remembered my birthday!" she exulted.

"Of course! Did you think I'd forget your sixteenth?" Beaming, he handed her the box. "Open it."

"Oh, Father," she said, pleasure bubbling up inside so that she could hardly speak. Lifting the lid, she gasped. There, folded, was the ruffled dress from Hank's General Store. Gingerly she held it up to herself, twirling about. "How did you know I wanted this?"

"Well," he said, his beard shifting slightly with his broad smile, "a certain Irishman whispered a secret in my ear!" He moved near her, placing his laced hands behind her neck, his forehead almost touching hers. "Sixteen years old!" he murmured, his eyes shining with admiration. "I can't believe you're still the same little girl I used to dawdle on my knee. I remember when you learned to walk. You were everywhere, upstairs spilling Mother's face powder, downstairs cuddling Tuffy."

He walked to the fireplace mantel and faced her. "You were always a delight to us, Julie." He chuckled. "Even when you climbed trees, fell off your horse, and went swimming in your pantaloons! You never sat still for more than ten minutes! Now," he ordered, clapping his hands, "get dressed in your party gown. We're having guests in half an hour!"

Her eyes widened. More marvelous surprises? "Guests?" she asked. Was it only an hour ago she had fought back tears and tried to forget her lonely birthday?

"Yes, I invited Samuel, Dylan, the Effertons, and the Morans. Even Hiram Harper. I could hardly leave him out when his nephew will be here."

"And I'd thought you'd forgotten! Thank you, Father!" She felt buoyantly happy. "I'm the luckiest girl in the world," she exclaimed, feeling her pink cheeks glow. "The only thing that would make this evening perfect would be to have Mother here!"

Jay Fulton sobered. "Yes, I know. I miss her, too, but she'll be home this month." His gray eyes soon had silver lights dancing in them again. "And you have a letter from her."

Eagerly, she moved forward, but he held up his hand to stop her. "It's to be read at your birthday party only. Now, upstairs with you! Put on your birthday dress and get

101

ready to have a wonderful evening!"

Dashing upstairs, she didn't see Michael until he stepped in front of her. His red hair was slicked down, and he wore a blue shirt with a black string tie.

"How handsome you look, Michael! Did you get dressed up just for your little sister?"

"Just for you, Julie. After all, it's a special birthday party for a special sister." From behind his back he pulled forth a box, handing it to her.

"Michael!" she gasped, taking the box. "You remembered! No wonder you've been so secretive all week. How could I have thought you and Father would forget?"

"Not on your life." He cocked his head to one side and placed his hands on his hips. "Want to peek inside?"

Laughing, she flung off the top. Her eyes grew big, and she couldn't help gasping. Carefully, she took out a white kid leather shoe. Its high top was decorated with jet beads along scalloped edges.

"Look inside the shoe," Michael urged.

From the heel, she pulled out a pair of white stockings. Unbelieving, she shook her head. "These must be made of silk," she said joyfully. "And the shoes! Where did you find such beauties?"

"Sent for them," he replied matter-of-factly, "all the way from Chicago." He rubbed his chin. "For a while I didn't think we'd get them. No trains were coming through. But yesterday on the Omaha run, my package arrived, just in time. But," he added sternly, "you won't be on time for your own party unless you get dressed!"

"Michael, I love you." Impulsively she threw her arms about him and kissed him. Then she hurried to her room. She was going to put on the most beautiful dress this side of the Mississippi.

Coming down the stairs, with all the guests assembled, Julie felt like a fairy princess. The soft chiffon swished gently about her silken-sheathed ankles. The softly ruffled collar was so feminine, and the pink fabric of the dress made her cheeks look dusty rose. Tiny green leaves cascaded down the side of her full skirt and decorated her wide scooped neckline. She had even taken an extra garland, a small one, and entwined it in her hair. The vivid green contrasted sharply with her rich, auburn hair.

For an instant, the memory of wearing this same dress in Hank's Store came back to her. After her horse trough dunking, she remembered how she yearned to own this delicate dress she was now wearing. Even then, however, she realized she had no place to wear it, and, besides, she had no boyfriend. Smiling, she stepped down the steps, aware of everyone's eyes on her. Just look at me now, she thought, a scant four months later.

Dylan was the first to rush forward and proudly escort her to the table where Mrs. Moran stood by the white cake she had baked. After Mrs. Moran had cut the cake and handed the first piece to Julie, she said, "For the loveliest sixteen-year-old in Crooked Branch and," the angular woman smiled, "in all Utah, for that matter."

Mrs. Efferton poured the coffee, and everybody wished her a happy birthday. After the cake and coffee, Mr. Moran opened his fiddle case and removed the stringed instrument. Standing in the corner by the fireplace, with Michael at his side, Mr. Moran struck up a lively tune.

The rug was rolled back, and the dancing began.

After a number of spritely polkas and Irish jigs, the musicians changed the tempo, slowing to a waltz. Samuel asked her to dance, gently holding her as they moved to the sweet strains. "I've never seen you looking more beautiful, Julie," Samuel said in a low voice. His eyes, amused and warm, took on the sheen of polished mahogany. "If you weren't spoken for, I'd sweep you off your feet and carry you away." With these words he swirled her about in a long gliding step.

The intoxicating music made Julie's head spin. Her hair fanned out behind her, and her spirits soared. "Samuel," she said, with a laugh, "you always make me feel so special."

His arm tightened about her waist. "You'll always be special to me, Julie."

The music stopped, and for one heady moment she lost herself in Samuel's warm, serious eyes.

Coming off the floor, they met Dylan, who handed each of them a second cup of steaming coffee. "Samuel," he bantered, "you *do* remember that Julie's my girl, don't you?" He playfully jostled Samuel in the ribs.

Samuel, holding his cup steady, smiled at Dylan. "How could I forget?" he asked lightly.

Everyone stopped talking when Jay Fulton tapped a spoon against his glass. "Miss Julie Fulton," he announced, "tonight is for you." He motioned with his hand. "Please come forward and take this seat of honor." He held out a chair for her.

Glorying in this moment of her sixteenth year, a new threshold of life, she gazed about at her good friends. Could life be any sweeter? In front of her were a number of boxes, all tied with ribbon.

"Before you open your presents I think you'd like to read Mother's letter," her father said, handing her an envelope.

Silently Julie scanned the contents:

Dearest Julie,

This will reach you on your sixteenth birthday. How I long to be with you on such a special occasion. But, my dearest, it won't be long. Granny Ruth is walking, so I'll soon be boarding that train for Crooked Branch.

For this birthday I've been saving a surprise for you. A pair of your great-grandmother's pearls, once belonging to Matilda Ann Fulton. Wear them in good health, my darling. They'll only enhance your beauty. I'm so proud to have a daughter like you!

With my deepest affection and love,
Mother

Julie's father moved behind her, fastening the clasp on the string of pearls. They gracefully fell over the shamrock that Dylan had given her and that she always wore. Tears glistened in her eyes as she touched the lustrous pearls.

"Here, here," her father said gruffly. "No tears. Look! You have other gifts to open."

With a sniffle and a smile, she opened each one. She couldn't believe the lovely things that her friends had given her. From Dylan a pair of leather riding gloves; from Samuel an ivory-handled fan; a velvet handbag from the Effertons; an umbrella from the Morans;

and finally, Hiram Harper casually handed her a gilt-threaded bolt of brocade. For the first time she noticed he had his arm in a sling.

The entire evening Hiram had worn his frock coat carelessly thrown about his shoulder so she hadn't noticed he'd been hurt. "What happened?" she asked incredulously.

He chuckled. "You were too busy dancing when I told my story. Ben Garner, one of my stagecoach drivers, and I were out inspecting a trail when a bunch of Cheyenne attacked us. They pulled me off my horse, and I landed on my shoulder." He patted his ample middle, barking a laugh. "With all this bulk I landed heavily. Ben fired his rifle and scared the Indians away. Fortunately it was only a broken arm I suffered. I could have been killed!"

"How awful!" she exclaimed, but she couldn't say any more. Her throat tightened, and suddenly, even at her splendid party, a tremor of premonition chilled her. These confrontations with the Indians could end only in bloodshed.

Chapter Eleven

On March twentieth, a dark and rain-swept day, the message Julie had been waiting for came through:

> ARRIVING ON THE FIVE O'CLOCK TRAIN
> MARCH TWENTY-FIRST.
>
> LOVE,
> MOTHER

Tomorrow! Her heart leaped. At last Mother was coming home. Julie couldn't wait. That afternoon she'd clean the house until it shone. She'd plan the menu for tomorrow and fix two things for sure — she'd bake an apple pie and roast a chicken, her mother's favorites.

All at once the office door opened, and a gray

mist swept into the room. Nell Brannigan lowered her blue-fringed parasol. "I want to send a telegraph message," she said in her husky voice, crimson lips smiling widely. "The name is Julie, isn't it?"

She smiled, too. "Yes, Julie Fulton."

"Julie. That's a pretty name." She whipped off her ermine-trimmed cape and perched on the edge of the desk. Her black dress, with its sequined bodice and white ostrich feathers on each shoulder and around the hem, hugged her figure. "I want you to send this message to Mary Brannigan in Chicago."

From beneath one long, black sleeve she extracted a piece of paper, unfolding it and handing it to Julie:

SENDING ENVELOPE WITH THREE HUNDRED DOLLARS. ON TRAIN NUMBER SIXTEEN, FRIDAY.

NELL

"Three hundred dollars!" Julie blurted out. "That's a lot of money. Is Mary Brannigan a relative?" she asked before she could stop herself.

Nell didn't seem to mind the question. "She's my mother," she said, her black eyes snapping. "Mary Brannigan has criticized me ever since I was a girl." Nell shrugged her shoulders. "Still and all she's my mother, and she needs the money." She laughed bitterly. "She doesn't like my owning a saloon, but she does like the money."

Julie gazed at Nell admiringly. She was a flamboyant woman who certainly knew how to wear a glittering dress. She looked quite spectacular.

"Your mother's a nice person, Julie," Nell said. "You're lucky. Rosie has never once snubbed me." Her violet-shadowed eyes studied Julie. "But you're pretty nice, too." She laughed throatily. "Well, it's time for me to go to work!" She stood, the white-feathered hem swirling about her black lace stockings.

"At noon?"

"Yes! Those railroad men don't care what time it is as long as the saloon is open." She flung her cape around her. "The fellows say you're very good at this job, Julie."

"They do?" Julie glowed at Nell's words.

"Indeed they do!" Nell responded crisply. She leaned over, winking. "I've seen you with Dylan O'Kelly. You couldn't ask for a better husband. If I were you, I'd grab him!"

Julie blushed, but answered her as matter-of-factly as she could. "He is nice," she said. "But I'd like to work for a while first, Miss Brannigan." She wondered why she was confiding in a virtual stranger, but Nell was easy to talk to. "I just had my sixteenth birthday, you know."

"I know," Nell said, a smile lurking in her dark eyes. "At sixteen I'd already worked as a waitress for a year."

Julie didn't quite know how to reply. Why was Nell advising her to marry Dylan when she herself was unmarried and had worked all her life? Julie speculated on whether Hiram Harper would ever ask Nell to marry him. She was startled when Nell mentioned his name.

"Hiram's expecting me, Julie, so I've got to run." She lifted her fur hood over piled-high curls.

"Unless," Julie said teasingly, "he's way-laid by Indians again and breaks his other arm."

Nell snorted. "Indians! Don't be ridiculous, Julie. I shouldn't be telling you this, but he fell down the stairs in the saloon."

Julie's eyes opened wider. "You mean he wasn't attacked by the Cheyenne?"

Nell, hands on hips, threw back her head, laughing. "Oh, no." She sobered, giving Julie a sidelong glance and placing a well-manicured finger across her lips. "But don't tell anyone. It sounds more heroic when Hiram says his arm was broken in a tussle with the Indians." She nodded and grinned. "You'll keep his little secret, won't you, Julie?"

"But, Miss Brannigan, that's dishonest,"

Julie protested uneasily. "His story casts more hate on the Cheyenne. Why would he want to do that?"

"Well, that's the story Hiram's telling." Nell shrugged. "And if it means that much to his image, I'll go along with his little white lie."

It was more than a little white lie, Julie thought with a flutter of apprehension. Hiram's story was wicked and hurt the Indians. She pressed her lips together, not certain what she was going to do, but at least she hadn't promised Nell that she wouldn't divulge Hiram's lie.

"Good-bye, my dear. Thanks for sending my message." With a wave of her mesh-gloved hand Nell opened the door.

Brightening, Julie forgot about Hiram. She liked Nell. It mustn't have been an easy life for her all these years. " 'Bye, Miss Brannigan. I hope I see you again."

"Unlikely." Nell gave a chuckle. "I don't go to the same social functions you're invited to." She was out the door before Julie could answer.

The next day dawned windy and gray. Julie went to the telegraph office. She was blissfully happy. This afternoon Mother would be home! It would be wonderful to see her again. She wondered if this would be her last day on the job. Surely her mother would want to rest up from her trip for at least a day or two.

After a busy morning Julie decided to take Cinder out for a brief run to Devil's Canyon. True, the weather wasn't ideal, but she couldn't just sit and wait for the five o'clock train! The March wind was an early sign of spring, and so was the melting snow. Cinder hadn't had much exercise for several months, and Julie yearned to see her secret haven again.

Saddling the mare, she rode through Main Street, past the depot and up a winding trail until she reached the suspension bridge. She stopped to survey the rocky terrain, most of it still snow-covered, but some of the upper reaches barren.

Dismounting, she tethered Cinder to a branch and eyed the swaying bridge with a shiver of trepidation. Did she dare venture across it in this wind? But she had come too far *not* to cross it. "Cinder," she said aloud, "maybe I shouldn't have taken you up here on such a blustery day. Look," she said, tying her to a low-hanging limb, "I'll go over the bridge and hike to my mountaintop and be back before you can flick your ears twice."

With these words Julie slowly picked her way across the walking bridge. Once she glanced down below at the roaring spring water gushing over the rocks, and her grip tightened on the hand rope. The stream, far below, had become a raging river.

Once across the footbridge, she hurried thankfully to the icy ground. A light rain began to fall, and an ominous roll of thunder growled in the background, punctuated by a jagged streak of lightning.

Suddenly a deafening crash splintered the darkening sky. Should she turn back? She half smiled. Since when did a little lightning and thunder stop Julie Fulton? She exulted in the rain splashing across her face. All winter she'd waited to see her secret haven. She was too near to turn back. She wouldn't stay long, but she had to see if it remained as she remembered it.

She trudged against the gusts of wind, the rain pelting her face. The drizzle had turned into a steady downpour. The booming thunder and flashing lightning no longer thrilled her.

Frightened, Julie began to consider turning around. She realized now that it had been foolhardy to attempt to climb to the top of her mountain in such a deluge. The wind became a gale, bending the saplings double. The path quickly became a quagmire. A pine branch tore free, whipping across the ground in front of her. Her heart lurched. How could she ever get back over the footbridge? Poor Cinder! In her first real outing of the season she was tied out in this wind and rain.

A crack of lightning caused Julie's spine to go rigid. She hurried back toward the footbridge, but the mud sucked at her boots, holding her back. The sky was green-black with charcoal clouds scudding furiously eastward. Lightning frequently stabbed the eerie darkness. Her stomach clenched tight. There wasn't a doubt in her mind. She must get back at once!

Back she flew over the twisting path, slick with mud and rivulets of water. Twice she stumbled and fell, but heedless of the wet muck covering her from head to toe, she scrambled to her feet and kept running. Panic welled up in her throat when she thought of the dreaded footbridge.

Coming to the edge of the canyon, she cried aloud, her nails biting into her flesh. One of the guy ropes that braced the bridge had snapped, and the bridge was heaving up and down like a bucking bronco. How could she even think of crossing it?

As she fearfully watched, the second guy rope ripped in two and the bridge burst free, lashing back onto itself and shattering against the opposite stone canyon wall. There it hung, swinging back and forth like a bedraggled trailing vine.

Stark black terror washed over Julie as she stared through the driving rain at the nearby train trestle. There was no way back to Crooked Branch except the match-stick-like structure on which the narrow track ran.

All at once, as she stared in horror, several crossbeams broke free, careening to the water below. The entire trestle swayed. How could a train ever cross the weakened bridge, Julie wondered miserably. The terrible awareness of what would happen swept over her trembling body. The train's weight would cause the collapse of the trestle, plunging the train onto the canyon floor.

Gritting her teeth, Julie rushed toward the trestle, her breath coming in spasmodic gasps. More wooden beams parted, plummeting downward. The wooden bridge moved as if it were alive. It looked as if the whole structure would fold up like a house of cards and crash. She *had* to get back to the telegraph! She must warn the engineer. She tried to hold on to her fragile control. Her mother was on that train!

She knew the trestle was designed with the ties far apart to discourage anyone from crossing it, but this was the only way back now. If only she had a lantern to warn the oncoming five o'clock. What time was it now? Three o'clock? Four? Four-thirty? A sob tore at her throat as she raced forward.

Arriving at the trestle, she took a ragged breath. The fifteen-hundred-foot trestle stretched ahead of her as if it were ten miles long! Gingerly, she stepped onto the first plank. Since there were no handropes to cling to, as on the footbridge, she sank down on all fours.

Crawling forward, testing her weight as she inched ahead, her heart hammered violently in her chest. She desperately wished she could turn back to wait out the storm. But if she went back to the safety of the ground, the train was doomed. A high moan penetrated the blackness. Was that animal sound coming from her?

The soaking rain drenched her, and huge drops of water clung to her eyelashes. As she groped forward, grasping one slippery tie after the other, she couldn't help seeing, in the intermittent lightning flashes, the blue-black torrent below. The waters boiled and thrashed like some great sea monster that awaited her fall just so it could devour her!

She placed her left hand on a tie ahead. Suddenly the sodden plank tore free, and one arm plunged into space, dangling over the abyss, causing Julie to lurch far to the left. Her scream was lost on the tearing wind.

Chapter Twelve

WITH one hand Julie desperately clung to the rail. She struggled furiously to right herself, but the iron rail was cold and slippery. Once her clutching fingers slipped, but she held on. With a superhuman effort she hoisted herself back to safety. Moving with great caution, she slowly and carefully balanced on all fours.

Julie gasped for breath. She didn't dare look down. After a brief respite she tried to move, but she couldn't prod her limbs forward. She was frozen to the spot. How long she remained huddled over the broken tie, she didn't know, but Julie was certain of one thing — she was *scared*! Her whole body trembled when she thought of how close she had come to plunging to her death.

A bolt of lightning galvanized her into action. Creeping forward, she tried to see the far end of the trestle, but it was impossible with the rain slashing across her face. If only she could stop shaking!

At one point her heavy wet skirt caught on a splintered tie, and she almost lost her precarious balance. But after a terrifying moment, she tore the sodden wool loose and proceeded. Because the slick ties were treacherous, she had to move deliberately. It was difficult to keep her hands from slipping. Twice the howling wind nearly toppled her over the edge, but when the blast blew against her, she flattened herself, lying face down, motionless. She gripped the rail so tightly her fingers ached. In the subsiding intervals of the gale, she started her arduous ordeal again.

Placing one hand in front of the other, she painstakingly progressed. She must reach the other side! What if the five o'clock train came roaring down on her? Then she'd be too late to save either herself, her mother, or the locomotive!

Julie's nerves throbbed, and her tired muscles screamed from the constant battle against the storm. Desperation spurred her on.

For a moment, an image of Dylan shimmered on the wet rail. The memory of his sweet embrace swept over her. If she ever needed his comforting arms around her, it was now!

Peering into the darkness, she imagined she saw a glimmer of light. It flickered, then was gone. Was she nearing the end of the trestle?

Suddenly there was a crack of splintering wood, and more buttressing supports flew out from beneath her. The bridge shivered and sagged! Would it continue to support her? Doggedly she went on. Right knee, left hand, left knee, right hand. Keep moving, she thought, clenching her teeth. Don't stop. She desperately wanted to see her mother alive — to see her father, Michael, Dylan, and Samuel again. She prayed for strength, but she was tiring fast.

Was that the "stop work" five o'clock whistle she heard? She prayed it was only the whistling wind!

At last she crawled off the swaying trestle, touching the rocky face of Devil's Mouth Canyon. A cry of relief burst from her lips. She had safely reached the other side!

Sprawling across the stony ground, she sobbed with relief. But this was no time for tears. She would have time to rest later.

Even though she ached in every joint, she was determined to finish the job. Wearily she staggered to her feet, but her knees gave way and she fell. Quickly, she struggled to her feet again. Nothing, she told herself stubbornly, was going to keep her from reaching the depot and the telegraph! A cracking, shivering crash rose to a crescendo above the storm. Wheeling about, Julie watched in horror as the entire trestle, moving as if in slow motion, caved in. The structure was gone, and where once had been a bridge, only a black void existed. Julie could barely believe she'd made it across.

Half stumbling, half running, she reached Cinder. The rain-soaked mare stamped and twitched her tail at Julie's touch. Clambering on Cinder's back, Julie urged her forward. Down the hill, the surefooted horse picked her way. Cinder's ears were pricked as if she knew she was on her way home. Julie had to hold the mare back, for despite the lessening rain, one misstep would plummet them to the bottom of the canyon.

At last Julie reached Crooked Branch. Never had the little town's wavering lights been so beautiful! Kicking Cinder to a gallop, she bent low, clinging to her horse like a burr. Her heart soared when she glimpsed the depot through the dripping trees.

Suddenly a train whistled. Had it already left Bear River Pass, only five miles east of Crooked Branch? Her throat closed and she couldn't breathe. The train didn't stop at Bear River Junction, but if the telegrapher was on duty he'd flag it down.

Rushing into the station, Julie was astonished to see her father and Michael. Of course. Why *wouldn't* they be here? They were waiting for Mother! But they didn't know about the trestle. No one knew!

"Julie!" her father exclaimed, startled to see her so bedraggled and sweeping her up in his arms. "Where have you been?"

"Julie!" Michael said, putting a strong hand on her arm. "Thank heaven you're safe. We've searched everywhere for you!"

Her father's arms and Michael's closeness felt comforting, yet she pushed them away. "The trestle!" she gasped. "It's collapsed!"

"No!" Jay whispered, his ruddy face suddenly ashen.

She touched her forehead, feeling dizzy.

"Sit down, Julie," her father urged. "Hurry!" He led her to the telegraph.

"Send out an SOS! Don't waste a minute!" Michael said urgently, patting her weary shoulders. "You can do it. Hang on!"

Shaking her head to clear it, her fingers clicked out the SOS. Then she tapped out the message:

TRESTLE COLLAPSED BETWEEN DEVIL'S
MOUTH CANYON AND BLACK MOUNTAIN.

Breathlessly, Julie waited for a confirming click of the keys. Silence. Had the telegrapher left? With trembling fingers she repeated the message.

All at once came the welcome answer:

LANTERN MAN DISPATCHED TO WARN
TRAIN.

"Thank goodness," Julie murmured just
before she pitched forward, sprawling across
the table. The last thing she remembered before she fell into a deep sleep were gentle
hands that seemed to be lifting her and carrying her to safety.

When Julie awoke, she was in her own
bed, sunlight streaming through the window.
Her parents were gazing down on her. Rosie,
with hands folded in front of her, leaned
over her daughter.

Tears sprang to Julie's eyes. "Mother,"
she said weakly. "You're alive!"

"Yes, darling. I'm alive." A soft smile
played about her lips. "Now, hush, rest." Her
mother wrapped her arms about her and
rocked Julie back and forth. "I owe my life
to you."

"How-how did you get over the canyon?"
Julie asked.

"Hiram Harper's stagecoach," she answered, sitting back.

Julie admired the strength underlying her
mother's beauty. "He sent the stage to pick
you up?" she questioned.

"Yes, me and the train crew," Rosie continued, tucking a wool blanket about Julie. "The coach went around the Old Mountain Road, crossing at Bear River Bridge. I only arrived home an hour ago." She pushed back a strand of black hair, and although there were deep rings under her eyes, her smile was glorious, wreathing her face in a pinkish glow.

For one whole day, Julie stayed in bed. She hadn't realized how exhausted she was. But the next morning she rose. The house was silent. Everyone had gone off to work. How quickly things had returned to normal.

Brushing her thick hair and putting on her green pleated skirt with a plaid shirt, she decided to visit her mother. Was it only yesterday she had been on a swaying trestle? Or was it the day before? She had lost track of the hours. But now, oh, now, she thought joyfully, how wonderful it felt to be alive. With a big, jaunty ribbon she tied back her hair. Downstairs she threw her navy cape around her slender shoulders and hurried outside.

"Julie, love!" Dylan called, coming up the path.

"Dylan!"

Holding Julie close, Dylan twirled her about. Laughing, she remembered her thoughts when she'd been caught in the storm and how she'd believed she'd never feel the comfort of Dylan's powerful arms again.

And now here she was, in his embrace!

"You don't know how grand it is to see you, Julie, me girl," he said jubilantly. Then he stopped and gazed into her eyes. "How close I came to losing you!" When he kissed her, she felt a warm glow.

Suddenly he grabbed her hand. "Come on, me Irish colleen! I've a surprise for you!"

Puzzled, she broke into a run to keep up with him.

Reaching Hank's General Store, an Irish band struck up a stirring march, and Jack Casement himself stood on the wooden platform. There beneath the flag was a banner that read:

THREE CHEERS FOR JULIE FULTON!

Astounded, Julie walked through the crowd. Everyone either wanted to shake her hand or pat her on the back. Tears moistened her eyes and her heart filled with happiness. Never had she been so thrillingly surprised!

Jack Casement motioned her forward to a chair on the platform. She sat alongside Dan Casement, Michael, and her parents.

Jack quieted the crowd, holding up his hands. She was still so dazzled by this adulation that she scarcely grasped certain phrases in Jack's speech: "the heroine of the Union Pacific. . . . Saved six lives. . . . Risked her own life. . . ."

Loud applause punctuated his sentences.

Again he held up his hand: ". . . the grateful citizens of Crooked Branch award her the Railroad Medal of Honor for unsurpassed valor." More clapping and whistles. Jack Casement stepped back, indicating she should move beside him.

The cheers resounded louder than the beating drum. Surely Mr. Casement must detect her pounding heart as he pinned the ribboned medal on her cape. The silver glinted in the sun, and the red ribbon shone brightly against the dark blue wool.

"Speech! Speech!" yelled the crowd.

Julie looked hesitantly at Jack Casement, who nodded vigorously. "Go on, Julie. They want to hear your voice."

"Thank you all," she said simply. "I was lucky to be where I could warn the train. From the bottom of my heart I thank each and every one of you!"

More cheers. Then Dylan leaped up onto the platform and kissed her, much to the glee of the onlookers. Samuel congratulated her, holding her hand and shaking his head, as if he couldn't believe she was capable of such a dramatic feat.

Later, after supper, still basking in the town's warm wishes, Julie sat surrounded by her family, Dylan, and Samuel in front of the fire. Never had she felt such a contented coziness as she leaned against Dylan's shoulder.

"We're so proud of you," her father said, his eyes twinkling. "What are your plans for the five hundred dollars the railroad awarded you?"

"I'm not sure," Julie said thoughtfully. Then she glanced at Dylan. "Dylan thinks the Northern Pacific is a good investment."

"I agree," Jay said.

"You can't go wrong with railroad stock," Rosie added, serving a piece of devil's food cake to everyone. "I thought devil's food cake was appropriate for such an occasion," she said, chuckling, her cheeks shiny in the firelight. "After all, it was Devil's Mouth Canyon that turned you into our heroine."

"Samuel," Julie prodded, "you haven't said much tonight. Were you surprised when you heard about my adventure?" Her tone was half teasing, half serious.

Samuel ran his fingers through his wavy hair and shook his head. "Not at all. I still remember the Cheyenne and your wild ride." He chuckled. "As much as I downplayed it, that story is all over town."

She cocked her head, smiling impishly. "Speaking of the Cheyenne, has your uncle had any more run-ins with them?"

"No," Samuel said abruptly, as if to dismiss the subject.

Was he trying to hide something? Julie

wondered. But no, how could he know that Hiram had been at the saloon the night he claimed that Indians broke his arm?

"Well, I hope there's no more trouble with the Indians," she retorted.

"Hiram Harper won't let anyone forget he was attacked," Jay said, lighting his pipe. "He says he'll go bankrupt — says if the railroad doesn't get him, the Indians will!"

Dylan snorted. "Your Uncle Hiram will always land on his feet, Samuel. If you don't mind my saying so, Hiram's a bit of a conniver."

Samuel smiled, nodding. "I have to agree with you, Dylan, and I guess I know my uncle better than anyone."

For a moment Julie almost told the story of Hiram's broken arm and the blame he heaped on the Indians, but she decided this wasn't the time. Poor Samuel looked depressed enough.

Chapter
Thirteen

BY the end of March the adulation had sub-
sided, but Julie was still buoyed by the out-
pouring of love from the people of Crooked
Branch. Wherever she went she was greeted
with appreciative warmth, and her trestle
story was repeated many times.

Also by March, track gangs had stormed
down the Weber River into Ogden. Grenville
Dodge had just returned from Washington
where he had met with President Grant, now
the eighteenth President of the United States.
Grant had told Dodge that the terminal point
of the two railroads would be at or near
Ogden. The Central Pacific and Union Pacific
knew they had better set the stopping point
or the government would do it for them.

This meant that everyone connected with

the railroad was leaving Crooked Branch today. Most of the laborers, though, had gone on ahead with Casement's construction train. Father, Michael, Samuel, and Dylan had already gone to Ogden. The whole town, loaded on railroad cars, would be moved within twenty-four hours to where the new track was being laid. Crooked Branch would simply disappear, Julie thought sadly. Many of the buildings were made so they could be quickly knocked down and reassembled. Oh, a few broken-down shanties and garbage heaps would remain. And the graveyard, of course. This past winter forty-five people had died, and only six by natural causes.

Julie carried her valise downstairs, wondering how many of the mushroom towns between here and Omaha had come and gone. There were a few towns that remained permanently, like Cheyenne and Laramie, but for the most part, where towns had once flourished there were now only empty wooden shacks and litter.

Julie tied her bonnet ribbons under her chin and hurried to meet her mother at the station.

When they boarded the wooden passenger car bound for Ogden, Julie gazed down Main Street. The already empty buildings, their windows staring back at her like baleful eyes, looked as if they understood they were being abandoned.

The engineer gave two long blasts on the whistle — the train signal for moving forward. Julie stared ahead. Now the track laying would proceed at full speed, and nothing could stop the Union Pacific! The merging with the Central Pacific wouldn't take long, and the transcontinental railroad would be complete. A major transportation artery would unite this country — more than the peace after the Civil War ever could!

Former President Johnson's "stop work" order had been rescinded by President Grant. The Union Pacific workers were laying five to six miles of track a day. Sometimes, though, the spring thaws delayed their frantic efforts, especially when rails laid in winter's rock-hard ground sank deep into the spongy turf and had to be rebuilt.

Last fall the Irish Terriers had laid eight miles of track in one day! But they wouldn't be able to match that record for a while, no matter how eager they were to beat the Chinese, known as Crocker's Pets. Julie smiled, settling herself back on the horsehair seat, and remembered the challenge Crocker had issued last October. After the Irish Terriers had laid their fantastic eight miles, he had boasted that the Central Pacific could lay ten miles of track in a day. Unheard of! And when Dodge, of the Union Pacific, accepted the bet, he also accepted Crocker's terms. Ten thousand dollars to be paid to the

Central Pacific if they succeeded! No one, not even Casement's Irish Gandy Dancers, could lay that many miles of rail in a day! So the bet had lain dormant all these months. Now that completion was near, would Crocker revive the bet? Julie groaned inwardly. She hoped not. Enough bad feeling already existed between the Chinese and Irish without this bet coming between them.

Rosie broke in on Julie's thoughts, saying, "It was difficult closing the office today." She paused. "You know, Julie, in setting up the new telegraph station in Ogden, I'll really need your help."

"You will?" Julie asked eagerly.

"Yes, I want to cut down on working. Three days a week would suit me fine." Her face creased in a wide open smile as if she already knew the answer to her next question. "Would you mind working the other two days?"

"Oh, Mother!" Julie exclaimed, almost bouncing up and down. "I'd love it!"

"I thought you would," her mother said airily, with a sparkle in her eyes. "Then that's settled. We'll plan our working schedule when we arrive. I have a feeling this job won't last long." She squeezed Julie's hand. "Then it's back to Denver. Just think! We'll have a new house with all the modern conveniences."

Julie managed a smile, but the clickety-clack of the rails echoed in her head. She didn't *really* want to return to Denver. How could she leave Dylan? Besides, pushing west was exciting. It was where she wanted to make her future. She didn't want to stay in Denver. If she was going to invest her money in the railroad, she wanted to see its progress first hand!

Julie caught her breath as the train wound through the Wasatch Mountains. The canyons and rivers were absolutely beautiful. Arriving in Ogden, she viewed the city perched at the junction of the Weber and Ogden Rivers, with Mt. Ben Lomond and Mt. Ogden to the east. The purple majestic mountains towered over the town.

As the train puffed into the station, a huge procession greeted them. Flags, posters, a brass band, and cannons added to the wild welcome. One banner read: HAIL TO THE HIGHWAY OF NATIONS! UTAH BIDS YOU WELCOME!

Ogden, although larger than Crooked Branch, looked similar. There weren't as many saloons, but the town had the same makeshift appearance. Even the people walking the boardwalks were the same. Hank's General Store was in the center of town, and Hiram Harper had moved the Double H Stagecoach Line to the edge of town.

After unpacking, Julie looked over their plain clapboard house. It was almost the same

as the one they had in Crooked Branch —
three bedrooms, a dining room, living room,
and a large kitchen with a pantry.

In the kitchen Mother unpacked dishes,
but when Julie offered to help, Rosie told her
to tend to Cinder instead. After the trip, the
horse would need a good run. Nothing could
have pleased Julie more. The brakeman had
told her that after Cinder was unloaded,
someone would bring her directly to the
house. Julie hurried outdoors to wait.

The fir trees in the yard ran down beside
the path that led straight to Ogden's Main
Street. In the distance Julie caught sight of
a horseman bringing Cinder. Running to the
end of the lane, she stood by the gate.

"Julie!" Samuel called, "It was lonesome
without you!" He rode up to her and dis-
mounted. "I was at the depot when Cinder
was unloaded and insisted on bringing her to
you." He leaned down, giving her a peck on
the cheek. "It's good to see you." Then, as if
embarrassed by his truthfulness, he hurriedly
untied Cinder from behind his own horse,
handing the reins to Julie.

"And I've missed seeing you, Samuel," she
said lightly. "You look wonderful!" And he
did, too, in his jaunty, tan plaid jacket and
his trousers tucked into his knee-high boots.
The wind played with his thick tawny hair,
and his clean-cut good looks were enhanced
by a deep tan. "How do you like Ogden?" she

queried, her mouth curving into a half-smile.

"It's another Crooked Branch." His shoulders moved slightly in his wool jacket. "Well, we won't be here that long anyway." He gazed at Julie, his brown eyes soft as velvet.

She smoothed Cinder's mane, flustered at the way Sam looked at her. She had to remind herself he was just a good friend. She cleared her throat. "The railroad's almost finished I almost hate to see it end."

Samuel laughed. "The way they're planning new western railways, the transcontinental is only a beginning!"

"Oh?" she asked pertly. "And are you going to become a surveyor with another railroad, Samuel?"

"I don't know," he replied thoughtfully. "I received an offer from Washington, D.C., to become chief surveyor in the U.S. Survey Office."

Julie wrinkled her nose. "After riding through these mountains, a Washington desk job sounds dull."

Samuel gazed about the hills and surrounding green forests. "Washington is very different from Utah, but it's far from dull, Julie." He touched a bright copper ringlet that had tumbled across her forehead. "You'd like it! But, then," he added, his eyes twinkling, "you could be happy anywhere."

She grinned, placing her foot in the stirrup. Samuel immediately rushed to assist her.

"I'd like to visit Washington one day," she conceded, "but there's so much to see and do out west. Right now," she said with a chuckle, "I only want to see Ogden."

"Mind if I ride along? I can show you a few highlights."

"I'd love to have you, Samuel. Let's go up that trail ahead." She pointed to a white ribbon that snaked up a hillside covered with pine trees.

"That's Rocky Knoll, a good choice," Samuel said, mounting his stallion and cantering alongside.

When they reached the hilltop, Julie was entranced with the small town below them. Ogden was nestled at the juncture of two winding rivers that seemed to hold the tiny town in a tight embrace. The buildings appeared pristine white against the blue of the rivers, but she knew they wouldn't look that way when she walked down Main Street.

"Samuel," she half-turned in the saddle, her eyes brilliant, "isn't it beautiful?"

"Almost as beautiful as you, Julie," Samuel said with a small smile.

Julie felt her face flush and hastened to change the subject, but, nonetheless, she was secretly pleased at his compliment. "Have you finished surveying the land around here, Samuel?"

"No, we're still going west. In fact, your father is in the field now, but he'll return by suppertime." He shook his head. "It's crazy. *We're* surveying the same land that the Central Pacific surveyors have already finished, and they're measuring land that we've covered!"

She sighed. "I wish they'd choose a stopping place."

"No one's in a hurry as long as the government is subsidizing each mile of track."

"I've heard President Grant is getting impatient," Julie said. "He's angry with both sides and their constant quarrels."

"It doesn't matter," Samuel added drily. "They still go on fighting. The railroad leaders are having a meeting next week, and they'll reach a decision then." He gave a low chuckle. "The golden spike has already been forged. It'll be a big day when that spike is driven in and the two railroads meet."

"Have you seen Dylan?" asked Julie, changing the subject again.

"Yes, his crew is working at the Salt Flats. They'll be in tonight, and I know he's eager to see you, Julie." Samuel abruptly mounted his horse. "I'd better get back. I promised to meet your father at Blue Creek Point."

"What about your uncle, Samuel? Is he settled yet?" Julie didn't know why she asked. She didn't really care about Hiram Harper.

Samuel nodded. "He moved the station last week, you know." Frowning, he added, "He has a few passengers, but the stagecoach runs are getting shorter the further west the railroad goes. I think he'd better pack up and move far away from the railroad before his business is completely ruined." He laughed. "But one doesn't tell Uncle Hiram what to do!" With a wave he wheeled his horse around and said, "See you later, Julie." Then he was gone.

Julie couldn't say she was sorry about Hiram. Samuel's uncle never cared about others. Now it was *his* turn to suffer a few reverses. She began to walk on the soft forest floor toward a grove of fir trees. She hated to see Nell Brannigan hurt, though. How could Nell be in love with Hiram? She guessed there was no reasoning with love.

She thought of Samuel, who once again seemed to be in love with her. What attracted her to Dylan instead of Samuel? Julie asked herself. Samuel was handsome, caring, and sweet, yet he didn't make her heart skip the way Dylan did.

A squirrel dashed across her path, skittering up a tree. Julie smiled as the squirrel leaped from one branch to another, and she decided to stay and explore. Perhaps she could find a secret place in Ogden, too, a quiet haven where she could think and be alone with the sky and the mountains.

She walked through the undergrowth. As the sun flitted in and out among the branches, she noticed that the maple trees had tiny spring buds. Julie's boots crushed a dead winter's twig underfoot. At last she found a secluded spot and sat down on a flat boulder.

She laced her fingers about one knee, leaned back, and gazed at the white clouds dotting the azure sky. Suddenly she heard someone crashing through the underbrush. Angry voices cut through the forest silence.

"I tell you, Frank, this will be the last time!"

She recognized Hiram's gruff voice and quickly ducked behind the rocks.

"I don't like it!" the one called Frank declared. "It's getting too risky!"

Hiram snorted. "Sure it's risky! But losing your job is risky, too! Now," he ordered, "you line up eight men and. . . ."

Their voices faded as they walked deeper into the woods.

Julie felt as if a cold hand had been placed on her spine. Whatever they were plotting, she had a strong suspicion it was against the railroad. Hiram was not going to lose his Double H Stageline without a struggle.

Careful not to make a sound, she crept out from her rocky niche. The sunshiny day had suddenly lost its sparkle.

Chapter Fourteen

JULIE quickly settled into the new environment of Ogden and the routine of her new job. She continued to go up on Rocky Knoll and was glad she didn't run into Hiram and his friend, Frank, again. Julie forgot the conversation she'd overheard in the thrill of seeing the railroad move onward. Excitement was in the air and bets were being taken as to the exact day that the last rail would be put in place. As the *Sacramento Bee* had stated:

The contest is between two great Corporations as to which shall construct and forever own most of the national highway.... They are coming together now on the home stretch and each is using the whip and spur to hasten forward everything connected with construction.

* * *

Julie felt she was doing her part. Along
with her mother, she, too, was busy as part-
time telegraph operator. The telegraph crew
had more than kept up with the tracklayers.
Now there weren't as many problems with
downed wires — the blizzards were over, and
so far no buffalo herds had rubbed against
the poles and toppled them. She was busier,
too, than in Crooked Branch, for more and
more trains were being dispatched. Besides
supply trains, tourists came flocking from
back East. These tourists wanted to see first-
hand the frontier where the Indians and railroad men lived, as well as the tracks moving
cross country like a great snake. Hunters
came, too, to shoot the buffalo, grizzly bears,
mountain deer, and antelope, most of them
with their new Sharp rifles.

In addition to these groups, journalists
poured in from their big papers in New York,
Chicago, Boston, Philadelphia, Pittsburgh,
Cincinnati, and Baltimore. The telegraph
wire was hooked up directly to Jack Casement's office so that he could be in constant
contact with the supplies and track conditions
in the rear. He also wanted daily commu-
niques from the Overland Telegraph Line out
of Sacramento. With this information he
knew exactly how fast the Central Pacific
workers were progressing. Julie and Rosie
were busier than they'd ever been.

She smiled. It was marvelous being needed and doing a good job. Julie hummed the popular Civil War tune, "When Johnny Comes Marching Home Again," for she felt happy. Today she was meeting Dylan at Blue Creek Point for a picnic lunch. Packing cold chicken and blueberry pie in a wicker basket, she paused. She hadn't seen much of Dylan lately, for he was busy and didn't come to the house as often as he'd done in Crooked Branch. Then, too, he was living in the bunk car of the construction train out of town.

Julie buttoned the tunic of her moss green riding suit that Samuel admired so much and examined the shine of her black boots. Yes, she was ready. One last thing, though, before she left. Examining herself in the mirror, she pinched her cheeks to give her face a rosy glow. With a shake of her head, she let her hair fan out and tumble freely about her shoulders. Just the way Dylan liked it.

The sunny day, caressed by a warm balmy breeze from the south, was beautiful. The blossoms on the apple trees stirred, and so did her heart. Julie saddled Cinder, feeling vivacious and pretty. To have a picnic with Dylan O'Kelly would add a sparkle to any girl's eye!

Riding out to Blue Creek Point she saw Dylan waiting for her. With his hands on his hips, he stood at the edge of the rippling creek, surveying the railroad tracks. In the distance a train gang ate lunch. That was one thing about Jack Casement. He always gave his men a full hour for the noon meal.

Catching sight of Julie, Dylan waved enthusiastically. "Julie, me darling. How grand you look!"

She smiled back at her Irish love. The sunlight glistened on his black curls and his lips parted in a dazzling display of straight white teeth. His skin, tanned by wind and sun, was stretched smoothly over his high cheekbones.

"I've found the perfect spot for our lunch," he grimaced playfully, motioning with his hand at the workers, "away from those roughnecks."

She grinned back at him. "Being part of that crew makes you a roughneck, too, doesn't it?"

"So it does!" he boasted, puffing out his broad chest. "But *what* a roughneck! Wait until I tell you!"

"Tell me what?" she asked, eyes dancing. "Do you have a secret?"

"Wait until we're seated under that tree," he said, helping her down from Cinder. "Look! We'll eat under those two oak trees. Isn't it the perfect spot?" he asked eagerly.

She nodded, catching her breath. Two tall trees arched over a grassy hillock decorated with yellow daffodils. The blue stream beyond made an idyllic setting. One would never guess a rough-and-tumble railroad town was only a few miles away.

"I see by the shine in those green eyes of yours, Julie, that you approve." He reached for the hamper and grabbed her by the hand. "Come," he added gently.

Laughing, she fell in with his merry mood as they raced toward the trees. What fun it was to be with Dylan!

"Guess what, me love?" Dylan said when they reached the picnic site and faced her. "I can't keep my good news to meself a minute longer!"

She smiled. Whenever Dylan was excited he lapsed into his Irish brogue. "What is it?" she questioned, her luminous eyes widening.

"I've been promoted to construction boss of Gang Nineteen," he said with delight. "Isn't that grand? Jack Casement says I'm one of his best workers. Says I'll climb the railroad ladder to success so fast it'll make me head swim." He threw back his head, crowing with laughter. "Ah, Julie, if he's right I'll buy you a big house, fine clothes, and expensive jewels."

"Dylan!" she exclaimed, catching his exuberant spirit. "I'm delighted for you!"

"Are you now?" he said half-mockingly, gazing into her eyes. "Delighted enough to rethink the question I asked a few months ago?"

"What question?" she teased.

The glint in his blue eyes matched the sunlight sparkling on the blue water. "You're sixteen now, and I'm a construction boss. . . . We can marry and have a good life. And," he said, gently poking her shoulder with his forefinger, "I won't be the construction boss of a train gang long, either. I'll move up to be boss of the whole shebang!"

Julie lowered her lashes. She wanted to be with Dylan, there was no question about it. But she wasn't ready for a wedding. Not just yet. Why couldn't he understand that?

As if reading her thoughts, Dylan gave her an amused look, lifting her chin with his fingertips. He kissed her on the tip of her nose. "I don't want your answer now, colleen, but I do want you to think about it. Your family will be returning to Denver soon. Then you'll need to decide if you want to remain here or go back with them." He touched her cheek. "Of course, I know you'll choose the finest Irishman west of the Adirondacks!"

She couldn't help but smile at Dyan's self-assurance. She wished she could say yes right now, but the words were trapped in her closed throat.

"Will you give me your answer soon?" Dylan persisted.

"I promise."

"Let's say you'll have your mind made up

by the end of the month? By then the railroad will be finished and I'll decide which railroad will be lucky enough to hire me."

"Oh, you will, will you?" she questioned with arched brows. "And what about me? Do *I* have a say in where we go? Maybe I prefer the Santa Fe ... or the Denver Western ... or the Pacific Northern!"

"Naturally you'll have a say-so," Dylan reassured her, cocking his head and smiling warmly. "But first things first. If you don't give me your answer soon, I may accept a railroad's offer and then," he shrugged, "it'll be too late. You'll just have to tag along behind me."

Her chin went up a notch. "We'll see about that," she said defiantly.

"Ah, you're a sight for these Irish eyes," he said. He held out his arms and she walked into his warm embrace. This was where she belonged! Why was she hesitating in becoming Mrs. O'Kelly? What was she waiting for? She only knew this was a big country and she'd only seen part of it. ... There was so much more to see and do!

"Hey, why so sober, little one?" Dylan asked, tilting up her face to meet his. His kiss was long and sweet. Finally he pulled away and said in a low voice, "We'd better eat."

"Yes, we'd better," she agreed shakily.

Laughing, she quickly unpacked the lunch.

"Come, my Irish Terrier. Being a construction boss you've got to keep your strength up and show your crew how the job's done."

As they were eating, Julie saw a man in buckskin riding alongside Jack Casement in the distance. Jack, as usual, was on his black stallion with a giant blacksnake whip coiled about his saddlehorn.

"Who's the visitor?" she asked.

"That bearded fellow? 'Buffalo Bill' Cody. He came in yesterday to negotiate a contract to furnish our crews with buffalo meat," Dylan explained. "He's only twenty-one and rode up from Abilene where he's been working for the Kansas Pacific. I've heard he's killed four thousand head of buffalo!"

"Four thousand!" she echoed in disbelief.

"Oh, Buffalo Bill's a crack shot, but it doesn't take much to shoot into a herd of buffalo. Those shaggy beasts are slow and stupid. They stand still, whether they're on train tracks or the prairie, and you can kill as many as you want. I don't see much sport in that." Dylan shook his head, helping her stack plates and roll up the tablecloth.

"Do you think Jack Casement will offer him the job?" Julie asked.

"I doubt it," Dylan replied. "Casement depends on his beef cattle herds that follow the crews." He smiled, holding her upper arms. His lips quickly brushed hers. "Got to run, darling. It was a wonderful lunch. Will you come out again and keep me company?"

She grinned. "Just try and keep me away."

With a chuckle, Dylan strode swiftly back to work.

Sighing, Julie turned to Cinder, not really wanting to go home on such a dazzling day.

Astride Cinder, heading for Ogden, Julie abruptly changed her mind, wheeling her mare about. She headed for the thickly wooded slope that led up to Rocky Knoll.

On the upward trail she paused to admire the new clumps of grass, green as fresh limes, sprouting at the trail's edge. A bird squawked nearby. Shading her eyes, Julie looked up. A hawk, wings spread, hovered in the clear sky.

On she rode, splashing across a small waterfall, until she reached the spot she'd rested in the other day. Dismounting, she walked through the trees, recognizing the rocky niche where she'd hidden and overheard Hiram and Frank. A crag towered above her. Curious, she began to make her way to the top.

By the time she reached the crest, she was out of breath and stopped at a row of scrub pines to rest. Gazing about at the rocky heights she was delighted to spot a cave. This would indeed be her secret place. Here there would be no intruders!

As she neared the vine-covered cavern the day suddenly became very still. Not even the scolding of a squirrel broke the silence. Peering into the cave's depths she could see nothing but a faint glint of light. Slowly she entered the dark, dank chamber.

As she advanced further into the noiseless cavern, her heels clicked on the flat granite stones of the cave floor. She put out her hand on the moist and clammy wall to steady herself.

A slight rustle lifted the hair on the nape of her neck. She froze. All at once, in the shaft of sunlight filtering from the ceiling hole, a bat swooped low, past Julie. She touched her cheek, feeling the air move from its flapping wings. Advancing further into the interior, Julie felt ridiculous. Why was she so afraid? It was only a harmless bat!

As her eyes grew accustomed to the gloom, she could make out the blackened embers of a cold fire. Someone had been here! She'd better leave before they returned! Backing toward the entrance she stumbled against something. Thrown off balance, she fell.

Leaping to her feet she spun about. But it was a harmless wooden chest trimmed with iron bands. Did someone actually live in this place?

Gingerly she lifted the lid. She sucked in her breath at what she saw. It was the purple-and-white Indian headdress that she'd seen before! Lifting out the trailing feathers, she frowned. Underneath were folded leather

Chapter Fifteen

BEFORE the intruder could catch sight of her, Julie hastily flung the Indian headdress back into the chest and quietly closed the lid. Then, as silently as possible, she hurried to the cave's nearest wall, away from the light.

The sound of heavy boots reverberated through the cavern. As the footsteps came nearer, Julie, terrified, spied a recess in the wall and quickly scrambled up into it. Lying on her stomach, she closely watched the intruder's every move. Julie's sharp eyes told her that the person in the cave was a man.

Unsuspecting that someone else was in the chamber with him, a shaggy, black-haired man lit a fire, then reached for a small bowl nearby.

What was he doing? Julie wondered as she

observed him use a stick to stir the bowl's contents. With his fingers he reached into the bowl, dabbing black paint on his cheeks and across his forehead. In the leaping firelight the dark swaths of color gave him an eerie, sinister appearance.

"Hello, Frank!" boomed a voice. *Hiram Harper*'s voice! Entering the cavern, the big man bared his teeth in a cynical grin when he came up to his companion. "Frank, you look more like a Cheyenne than Chief Red Deer himself!"

Desperately Julie tried to squirm deeper into the shallow shelf, but it was too narrow. There was no place else to hide. She wished she had some of that black paint to smear on her face for camouflage. She needed to become invisible.

"Ready for our last job?" Hiram inquired, squatting on his haunches in front of the fire.

"I suppose so," the man called Frank muttered, his eyes narrowing. "And this had better be the last time!"

"I said it was, didn't I?" Hiram snapped. He sighed in exasperation. "Now, if you want to keep your stagecoach driver's job and get that bonus of eight hundred dollars I promised you, you'll quit complaining and get this over with!"

Julie's eyes darted nervously from one man to the other.

"What if someone gets killed?" Frank's expression was resentful.

"No one will get hurt if you follow orders. Just start the rock slide to block the tracks," Hiram ordered, pushing back his wide-brimmed hat and pulling on his white beard. "That should delay supply trains for at least a week!"

"Yeah," Frank sneered, his brows drawing together. "I just hope I'm not caught."

"You won't be. You'll be on top of the hill and able to make your getaway before the dust clears." Hiram pulled out his pipe, holding it by the bowl and pointing the stem at Frank. "This will send Casement and his boys after the Indians beyond Salt Lake and buy us more time."

"I can't understand why the Cheyenne don't throw in with us," Frank said, wearing a puzzled scowl. "What are they waiting for?"

"I *told* you," Hiram insisted. "I talked to Red Deer, subtly of course, not implicating us, but Jack Casement has sold the chief on the idea of peace." Hiram snorted contemptuously. "Red Deer will have wished he'd stood up against the railroad when he's hunted down for something he didn't do!" He laughed nastily. "This is going to cost the railroad a pretty penny."

Julie clenched her fists. What a terrible man Hiram Harper was! He was willing to sacrifice men's lives in order to keep his precious line running. How greedy and rotten could you get? And how could someone like Samuel be related to Hiram? And how, for that matter, could Nell Brannigan be in love with him?

Strapping buckskin leggings over his tan trousers, Frank mumbled under his breath, "It's too dangerous. Why go through this masquerade? Why not just blame the avalanche on 'Crocker's Pets'?" He pulled off his boots and slipped into the moccasins. "Those Chinese caused a few avalanches themselves last month."

"No!" Hiram's staccato tone ripped through the air. "The Irish Terriers started the rock slides when they first worked near the Central Pacific crews, but the Chinese only took so much. When they retaliated with avalanches, killing three Union Pacific men, the Irish cooled their hot tempers and ended the dangerous game. There's been an uneasy truce between the two sides ever since."

He shook his head, tamping down the tobacco in his pipe. "No, Frank, I doubt if Jack Casement would believe the Chinese would start the fighting all over again. The Irish might, yes, but not the Chinese. Besides, neither side wants any more 'accidents.'" He tapped his temple knowingly. "I've thought this whole Indian thing through, Frank. Let *me* handle the plans."

"All right," growled Frank. "I'll do it your way."

"That's right. You will," Hiram said in an ominously gentle voice. "Don't you see? The railroad men will have to stop work and go up into the hills after the Indians. Every delay, every setback to the Union Pacific, means more money in our pockets!"

Frank lifted on his elaborate feathered headdress. Julie scrutinized him, realizing he didn't look much like an Indian up close. He was too thick around the middle, and his face was too fleshy. Although on that picnic day months ago, from a distance, she'd really been fooled! The image of Frank jumping onto his horse came back to her.

Suddenly she remembered the saddle on Frank's horse. Of course! Why hadn't she recalled that detail before? Indians always rode bareback. She bit her lower lip in frustration. If she had only thought of that earlier, perhaps she could have prevented the bitter anti-Indian feelings — perhaps even stopped the hatred that escalated more each day. Then, too, Nell had told her the truth about Hiram's broken arm. Nell had known he wasn't hurt in a skirmish with the Indians, so why had she kept silent?

Julie's mind was racing, but she decided she'd better concentrate on her perilous predicament. Somehow she had to escape and warn the train gangs of the avalanche! If she could sound the alarm, she knew Jack Casement would send out a crew with guns, and Hiram and his men would soon be hauled off to jail.

Julie wriggled uncomfortably. Wouldn't Hiram and Frank *ever* leave? They were conversing in low tones, and though she strained to hear, they didn't raise their voices in anger again.

Then, much to her relief, Frank slowly stood up. "Time for me to round up the boys," he stated flatly. "We'll finish the job as soon as possible. The slide will happen late this afternoon — at dusk." He smiled crookedly. "Then we can fade into the darkness."

Where, Julie wondered desperately, was the avalanche to take place? The rocky ravines and cuts through canyons were everywhere. How could Frank's men be intercepted if she didn't know where they'd strike? And she couldn't do anything while she was cornered on this ledge! Again she shifted her cramped muscles slowly and carefully so as not to make a sound.

"I'll come by your house later to report, and," Frank added with a leer, "to pick up my money!"

"Do that!" Hiram replied pleasantly. "No hitches this time, though. Don't let a teen-aged girl scare you away with her pistol."

"How'd we know when we tore up that track last fall it was a mere slip of a girl?"

Frank flared. Angrily he tossed a branch onto the fire, watching the flames blaze up. "I wish I had her here now! I'd like to throttle that red-haired troublemaker!"

Julie's blood chilled. If only Frank knew how close she was.

"Think you could handle her?" Hiram asked, a note of amused sarcasm in his words.

"I'd handle her all right," Frank said menacingly, his fingers curling in midair.

Julie shrank back.

"Ah!" Hiram said, cutting the air with his hand. "Stop worrying about Julie Fulton. She's an annoyance, but she won't bother us again. After all," he chuckled, "she's only a harmless girl."

Sudden fury hit Julie's eyes. Oh, she thought, glaring at Hiram and fervently wishing to see him caught and punished. A harmless girl, indeed!

"Get going, Frank!" Hiram ordered.

With a finger flick to his forehead, Frank left, his moccasins soundless on the stone floor.

Julie, after watching Frank depart, now stared at Hiram, willing him to follow. But the big man, using a twig that he held over the flames, lit his curved pipe. If only he'd leave so she could warn the train crews about the avalanche!

Instead of leaving, however, Hiram smoked contentedly on his pipe, staring into

the fire. It looked as if he had no intention
of going just yet. There was a contemplative
gleam in his cold blue eyes. What was he
thinking about? The Double H line? Nell?
The avalanche? She shuddered, taking a
deep ragged breath. If he didn't soon depart,
she'd never be able to move her sore muscles.

Hiram glanced about the cave. From her
darkened vantage point, Julie stiffened. He
was staring straight at her! Had he seen
her? No, she had to remember she was in the
dark. He had no idea she was only a few
steps away. How long had she been here?
Was it the end of the day? Was it getting
dark? Impatiently she watched Hiram puff
his pipe, the smoke spiraling into the air.

Finally he rapped his pipe on a nearby
rock, spewing the ashes across the pebbly
surface.

A wave of relief washed over her. At last!

Hiram wore heavy boots and waded right
into the small fire, stamping it out. Giving
a satisfied grunt, he placed his white hat
squarely on his head and stomped outside.

Was it safe to leave now? She straightened
her stiff legs, but in standing she loosened
a stone that fell. The sound echoed throughout the cave. She held her breath. Had Hiram
heard? Would he return? After a moment of
listening, Julie felt secure. Hiram had left.
No doubt he had gone back to Ogden to play
innocent. Oh, how she'd revel in bringing

him to justice! And she would, too. She couldn't wait to tell Jack Casement what Hiram was plotting.

Stealthily she tiptoed forward, almost afraid Hiram would reappear. She hesitated once, waiting a few seconds to be sure he'd have time to get down the hill. She vowed that after she'd told Jack Casement, she'd find Nell and tell her just what kind of man she loved. And Samuel. He must get away from his unscrupulous uncle. The sooner the transcontinental railroad was finished, the better. But an ugly thought crossed her mind. What if people linked Samuel with Hiram's betrayal just because he was living with his uncle? But, no surely people would be fair. It was plain to see Samuel's loyalty was with the railroad!

She moved toward the bright entrance. Good. The sun was still shining, which meant there was time to clear the crews out of the rocky defiles before the avalanche struck.

Pushing aside the vines, she stepped into the sun and hitched up her skirt in preparation for a swift horseback ride. But before she could take one step, a voice at her elbow purred, "Hello, Julie. Did you enjoy eavesdropping?"

Shocked, she spun about. She stared, speechless, at Hiram Harper! Although he smiled sourly, his pale eyes were like bits of glass. She whirled around to flee, but Hiram's

159

hand, quick as a snake's striking head, reached out and grasped her wrist.

He yanked her toward him, chuckling softly. "You're staying here with me, Miss Fulton!" Her senses reeled. She had been so close to getting away!

Chapter Sixteen

FRANTICALLY Julie tried to wrestle free from Hiram's iron grip, but it was impossible. "No tricks," he growled, twisting her arm viciously behind her back. He dragged her after him while she fought and clawed every step of the way.

When they reached a clearing surrounded by elderberry bushes, he halted. She glared at him, once more lashing out. She was panting wth exhaustion, but she knew if she could reach his face and rake him with her nails, she'd have a chance to run for freedom.

"Oh, no, you don't!" Hiram shouted, sensing her plan. He grabbed Julie's shoulders, shaking her until her head bobbed back and forth like a rag doll's. "I've had enough of you!"

All at once she ducked her head, biting his hand.

He bellowed in pain. "You witch!" he yelled, backhanding her across the face so hard that she tumbled into the dust.

"Don't move!" he thundered, towering above her. She cringed, thinking he was going to slap her again, but instead he examined his bleeding hand.

"You'd better get help for your hand, Hiram," she said matter-of-factly, rubbing her burning cheek. "They say a human bite is the deadliest of all!"

"Shut up!" he growled, whipping out his bandanna and wrapping it around the teeth marks. "So you were spying on us!" he sneered, a toothy smile flashing across his bearded face.

She defiantly looked into his glittering eyes, but inside quaked with fear. She longed to move her sore jaw. It felt as though he'd broken it, but she wouldn't give Hiram the satisfaction of knowing he'd hurt her. Staring at him, she wondered what he had in mind.

"Do you know what they *do* to spies?" he asked ominously.

She lowered her lashes, remaining silent.

"They *execute* them!" he crowed. Lifting his booted foot onto a rock, he observed her, shaking his head. "What am I going to do with you, Julie? You pose a problem. Quite a problem."

Her heart thudded as she squinted into the fast-sinking sun. If she didn't warn Jack Casement soon, it would be too late. She groaned inwardly. How many workers would be killed? And would *she* escape with her life?

"Now," Hiram continued smoothly. "I'll feel much better once you're tied up. You're too feisty for your own good!" He glowered at his bandaged hand. "And don't try anything foolish!" A look of fury crossed his face.

Her stomach knotted. He might do more than just hit her. In fact, she was certain he planned to kill her to save his own hide! How many other railroad "accidents" had he caused?

"I've got a lariat on my saddle. I won't trust you until you're tied up." He pointed at the narrow trail winding downward. "Head down there, Missy! And go slowly!" he warned.

Warily she rose to her feet. If she were going to run, she would need to do so before Hiram wore her down.

Down the steep path she went with Hiram directly behind. She glimpsed Hiram's horse tethered to an oak. Cinder was on the other side of the ridge. If she could only get to her horse, she knew she could outride Hiram. But how could she distract him? She could feel his hate-filled eyes boring into the back of her head.

Suddenly, an explosion tore through the air. Tree branches quivered, and the earth trembled beneath her feet. Of course! Today they were blasting in Tunnel Five.

Without thinking, Julie dashed and skittered down the hill. Once she lost her footing but regained her balance. She was going too fast. When she tried to stop her mad scramble by catching hold of nearby branches, she fell. Without losing her momentum for an instant, she rolled over several times. She scrambled to her feet. Rushing through the brambles and thick undergrowth to where Cinder was tied, Julie leaped on her back.

Hiram's roar of rage echoed up and down the valley. She could hear limbs being broken in his mad rush to apprehend her, but she didn't look back. "Go, Cinder, go!" she commanded, kicking her mare in the ribs.

She could hear Hiram's big stallion snort. She knew though, that not even Hiram's powerful horse would be as surefooted as Cinder.

Fleeing into the wind, hair streaming out behind her, she urged Cinder into a swift gallop. Pulling on the reins, she headed in the direction of the construction train west of town. She hoped she'd be on time, but the sun's rays were low and the sky was streaked with purple. Was she being pursued? She didn't dare to stop and listen.

If only she could reach the train crews, then she'd be safe! They'd believe her story, too. Her reputation with the railroad was secure. Hiram's definitely was not.

"Faster, Cinder, faster!" Julie urged. Dusk had fallen. Up ahead she could glimpse the flickering lights. Was she too late?

At last she came to Casement's train. She sped by the cars until she came to the last one. Leaping off Cinder's back, she burst into the office.

Jack Casement and his brother, Dan, were studying a model of a tunnel.

Astonished, Dan stared at her. Julie pushed back her hair, thinking how awful she must look — wild-eyed, hair flying, clothes torn, face bruised. But she didn't care.

"There's going to be an avalanche any minute!" Her voice cracked and she couldn't utter another word. Her throat was too dry.

"Are you crazy?" Dan Casement exclaimed.

"Now, wait a minute, Dan. I trust this young lady! After she saved our train from a collapsed trestle, I'd believe anything she tells us." He looked at her directly and crisply questioned, "Where's this avalanche going to take place?"

Tears blinded her. "I don't know," she stated lamely, helplessly flinging out her hands. "Hiram Harper and someone called Frank will start a rock slide along the tracks."

"When?" Jack Casement shot out.

"At dusk," she sobbed. "Now!"

Jack grabbed his hat. "Dan, you ride east and I'll go west. Warn any crews that are still working to get out of the cuts! And Julie," he flung his parting words over his shoulder, "go home!"

After the brothers had gone, she breathed in deeply and stepped down from the caboose. The workers up and down the tracks gave her a safe feeling. In the distance, a train gang trudged up the track. She prayed it was Dylan's, but when she heard their work song, she knew it was a Mormon crew.

Reaching her horse she wearily leaned against Cinder, then led her lathered horse away. "I'll walk, Cinder, and give you a rest."

Arriving home disheveled, Julie burst into the room. Her father, mother, and Samuel were seated before a fire, drinking a cup of ale. She ignored their questioning looks and hastily asked, "Have you seen Dylan or Michael?"

"They're not in from work yet? Why?" Her father's wide smile was replaced by a question of concern.

"It's Hiram!" She glanced at Samuel, not wanting to hurt him, but there was no easy way to avoid it.

Her mother led Julie to her chair. "Sit here, darling. I'll get you a cup of tea."

Julie smiled her thanks. Briefly she told them about the avalanche, about Hiram's capturing her, and her escape.

Rising, Samuel placed a comforting hand on her shoulder. "Julie," he murmured, "the side of your face is black and blue."

"Yes," she said ruefully, "your uncle hit me pretty hard."

A muscle rippled along Samuel's hollow cheek. "I'd like to get my hands on him!"

Julie shuddered. Frank had said those same words. Only he had been talking about *her*.

"I don't think Hiram will ever dare show his face in Ogden again!" her father said angrily. "If anyone needs to be tarred and feathered, he does!"

"Drink this," Rosie urged tenderly.

Sipping the tea that warmed her whole body, Julie felt better. The only thing that would complete her contented happiness would be to have Dylan and Michael walk through the front door. She would worry until they did.

Jay grasped his wife's hand. "I'm going down to the construction train, to wait for news." He gave Julie a twisted smile. "Maybe Frank got cold feet and didn't go through with the avalanche."

Rosie untied her apron. "I'm going with you, Jay," she said, her lips pressed together.

Jay chuckled. "I know that look of determination, Rosie, my dear. And," he said, "frankly, I'm glad to have your company." He turned to Samuel. "Why don't you stay here with Julie?"

Julie started to get up. "I want to go, too," she said, but her legs felt rubbery.

"Absolutely not," her father said, "not after what you've been through."

Samuel gently urged her back onto the chair. "I'm not going to let you stir. There's nothing you can do, and your folks will come back as soon as they have any news."

"We will," Jay said. "Come, Rosie."

Rosie admonished her daughter. "You'll help us by remaining quiet and resting. You don't realize what you've been through and what it's taken out of you. Will you promise to stay here?"

"I promise," Julie said reluctantly.

After her parents left, Julie leaned back in her chair, staring at the closed door. She had to admit it was a relief to be relaxing in her own home. A tingle of fear went up her spine when she remembered how close she had come to being elsewhere — maybe tied on a mountaintop or floating in the river.

Samuel offered her a plate of cookies.

Julie smiled, shaking her head. Samuel sank down on the cobbler's bench next to her. He took her hand, rubbing it gently. "It's good to have you safe, Julie."

Gazing gratefully at Samuel, she said, "Believe me, it's good to be here. Your uncle had a wild look in his eyes and," her voice quavered, "I think he intended to kill me."

"Poor Julie. There's no doubt about it. Uncle Hiram is mean-spirited when it comes to money." Samuel shook his head in disbelief. "I just didn't think he'd go this far."

"I don't understand Hiram," she said. "He even attacked you, Samuel, that day of our picnic."

"He wouldn't have hurt me," Samuel said confidently, but he rubbed his chin thoughtfully. "Why did he do this awful thing today? He could have sold the horses and coaches and retired in great style."

"He's so unlike you, Samuel." She patted Samuel's hand, knowing how this must hurt him. "It must have been difficult living in Hiram's house."

Samuel's eyes clouded. "There were some difficult times," he agreed, "but he could be a good man, too." He contemplated the fire. "I remember when he showed me Crooked Branch for the first time. We rode along the river, and he told me he was glad I'd come." He paused, then added wistfully, "He said he was lonely."

"Hiram, lonely?" she asked, unbelieving.

"Yes, lonely," Samuel repeated with a slight shrug. "But money was too much on his mind. Gold became an obsession. And now," his tone saddened, "it looks as if he'll be destroyed by it!"

For an instant Julie almost felt a twinge of sympathy for Hiram, but when she remembered how he'd slapped her and plotted to destroy the railroad, no matter who stood in the way, her heart hardened.

Samuel's handsome face kindled into a bright smile as he changed the subject. "Are you going to watch 'Crocker's Pets' try to lay ten miles of track next week?"

"Perhaps," she said hesitantly, "if everyone is all right here at home."

Samuel knew what she meant and said reassuringly, "Dylan and Michael are survivors! They'll be fine!" He cleared his throat and went back to the Central Pacific and the laying of the ten-mile track. "Crocker has actually set the date; April twenty-ninth is the big day. I think he was waiting for the finishing point to be established by both sides. Now that they've picked Promontory Point, Utah, he'll go ahead with the bet. Everyone will be watching. The crew will start at seven in the morning and stop at dusk."

"Dusk?" she echoed feebly, her mind wandering again. Dusk was when Frank was to have started the rock slide. It was long past dusk now. She wondered if the avalanche had taken place.

Samuel chuckled. "Crocker's men will never lay that much rail in one day — never," he said confidently.

She smiled at Sam, who was obviously trying to distract her. "Well, if Crocker wins, the Union Pacific will owe him ten thousand dollars!"

For a while they chatted pleasantly before the crackling fire, but the more time that passed, the more Julie worried. Where was everyone? Over two hours had passed, and still no word!

Finally, the door opened and her parents, along with Michael, entered. Julie's hands grew clammy. Where was Dylan?

Leaping to her feet, she dashed to Michael's side, kissing him. "Michael! I'm so relieved you're safe!" Stepping back, she asked her father, "Is Dylan all right?" Her mouth was so dry she could scarcely form the words.

Grimly her father shook his head, taking her hand. "The avalanche happened in Rattlesnake Gorge," he gazed sympathetically at his daughter, "where Crew Nineteen was working."

Her hand instinctively went to her throat. "And Dylan?"

Chapter Seventeen

WHEN Julie came to, she touched her aching head. Then she remembered! Dylan! He'd been caught in the avalanche! She looked up to see her mother hovering over her. There were creased lines about Rosie's eyes, which were as green and soft as new moss.

Pushing her mother's solicitous hand away, Julie shakily swung her wobbly legs over the side of the couch. "I must get to Rattlesnake Gorge!" she said in a tremulous voice.

"You'll do no such thing," Rosie said sternly. "There's nothing you can do. As soon as the men are dug out from the rock slide, they'll be rushed to the field hospital."

"As soon as they've been dug out!" Julie

whispered, clutching the shamrock Dylan had given her. "Oh, why couldn't I have warned them on time?" Agonizing regret assailed her. She moaned softly, her eyes filling with tears. "I pray Dylan is safe."

"I'd bet on it!" Sam said evenly. "He's too tough to keep down. I'm going to the hospital," he added. "When Dylan is brought in, I'll come and get you, Julie."

She grabbed his hand. "No matter if he's alive or," she choked, "dead."

Samuel swallowed with difficulty and glanced away.

Her hand tightened on his. "Promise you'll let me know."

"I promise," he whispered, his eyes suspiciously moist.

It was midnight when Samuel left, but no one made a move to extinguish the lamps or go to bed. Julie, miserably twisting her fingers, sat staring blankly into the flames.

At two-thirty in the morning, someone pounded on the door. Julie raced to answer it before anyone else.

Samuel, his fingers going around his hat brim, stepped inside and said quietly, "They've brought in Dylan."

Pulsing anxiety coursed through her veins. "Well," she asked nervously, "how is he?"

"He's still unconscious."

Color drained from her face. "I'm going to

him," she said firmly, tossing her head and daring her parents to say no.

Rosie nodded, getting Julie's striped shawl.

"I don't need a wrap," Julie said impatiently.

"The night air is chilly," her mother admonished, draping the shawl about her daughter's slender shoulders.

Without arguing, Julie pulled the fringed wool stole closer and left with Samuel.

When they arrived at the hospital tent, Julie was met by Dr. Nelson, who blocked her way.

"Dylan regained consciousness and now is sleeping," he explained. "I've given him something for the pain."

"How is he?" she asked anxiously. "Will he be all right?"

"He'll live," the doctor said cryptically.

She glowed with pleasure at the happy news, but the doctor's sober face and the way he pulled on his trim goatee wiped away her smile. "What is it?" she inquired fearfully.

"It's his legs, I'm afraid."

"His legs?" she asked sharply.

"Yes, Julie." He studied her, compassion in his intelligent eyes. "He tried to walk, but the pain was too excruciating. I examined him briefly and you must be prepared." He hesitated. "Dylan may never walk again."

A sinking feeling of despair shot through her, chilling her to the bone. Dylan unable to walk? Impossible! Not strong, easygoing Dylan. Not the man whose future was with the railroad and who was going to continue building them! Her fist went to her mouth to stifle a cry. Then, composing herself, she asked quietly, "May I stay with him? I want to be here when he wakes up."

The doctor nodded. Looking into Julie's strained, oval face, he was consumed with pity. "But only you, Julie. I don't want any more than one person here at a time." He turned to Samuel. "Go home, my boy, and get some rest. Both you and Julie look as if you were going to collapse at any moment."

"I'm fine," Julie lied, feeling a flutter in her stomach.

Samuel gazed at Julie and she took his arm. "Do as the doctor orders, Samuel. We've got to keep up our strength for Dylan." She smiled at him. "I'll take the first shift," she said as she gave him a little shove. "See you tomorrow."

"All right," he said, moving to leave reluctantly, "but I'll be here early in the morning."

"Tomorrow," she repeated softly, then hurried inside.

When Julie entered the large tent with its ten-bed capacity, she nearly let out a cry of anguish. Dylan, his black, tousled hair pressed against the white pillow, looked pale, and a jagged red gash ran down his cheek. He was so still, and even though he was asleep, there were lines of pain etched about his mouth. Tenderly she pushed back a curly ringlet that had fallen across his brow.

For the rest of the night she remained at his bedside. It wasn't until morning that he awakened.

Her eyes were closed when Dylan said, "Good morning, Julie."

Her lashes flew open. "Dylan!" she exclaimed, rising stiffly to her feet and leaning over him. "How do you feel?"

A glazed look of hopelessness darkened his face as he said heavily, "I'm all right." He studied her face. "Last night, did the doctor tell you I couldn't walk?"

She nodded, afraid to speak.

He reached down, grasping his legs. "My legs are numb," he said, his face contorted into an anguished frown.

"Dylan, sweet," she said, reaching out to embrace him, "you'll recover."

He turned his face away, paying no attention to her overture of love. "Leave me alone, Julie."

Pity stabbed her heart as she sat back, not daring to touch him again.

Still not looking at her, Dylan said in a muffled tone, "Go home, Julie."

"I-I want to stay with you," she begged, her voice suddenly cracking with sorrow.

"I know you mean well, Julie, but the doctor will be back soon." Again he said firmly, "You'd better leave."

"All right, Dylan, if that's what you want, but I'll come back this afternoon."

"Don't bother." His lips thinned and he lowered his eyes. "You've a job to do. That comes first!"

She said, smiling through the tears trembling on her eyelids, "You come first with me, Dylan." She took his hand. "And you always will!"

Unsmiling, he gently removed his hand from hers.

Sighing, Julie stood. She bent down and tucked in the blanket. Tenderly she kissed his forehead.

Dylan closed his eyes as if suffering from her touch.

With an overwhelming feeling of despair, Julie walked away.

Slowly she walked home, her thoughts in a turmoil. Going to her room, she lay down, but knew she wouldn't sleep. How could she? Her every thought focused on Dylan. What if he never walked again? She groaned, flinging an arm over her eyes. He'd never walk if he didn't try. He *would* try and he *would* walk, she resolved. She'd help him! Dylan was too high-spirited to languish in bed.

In spite of her agonizing thoughts, she drifted into a troubled sleep. She had a terrible dream. Samuel, carrying Dylan on his back, was running after her. Both boys, arms outstretched, tried to catch her. She ducked, running from them, and ran into Hiram, who held her firm.

When she awakened, it was late in the afternoon. Subdued voices from downstairs drifted up to her.

As she brushed her long hair, she stood at the head of the stairs, listening unabashedly. She had caught Dylan's name. Whatever they were discussing also pertained to her.

"The doctor's diagnosis is leg paralysis," Samuel said. "Even though his legs aren't crushed, he can't stand. The doctor says a spinal nerve might be severed. Chances are he'll be in a wheelchair the rest of his life."

"Poor Dylan," Rosie said sympathetically, her voice dropping. "Isn't there any hope?"

"Dr. Nelson did say it could be a temporary paralysis, so there's always hope, but we've got to remember that Dylan has been through a terrible ordeal — virtually buried alive for eight hours."

"What a tragedy. He's such a vibrant young man," Rosie answered.

"Maybe the doctor has had time for a more thorough examination," Samuel suggested. "I'm going to pay Dylan a visit."

"And I'm going with you, Samuel," Julie said determinedly, running downstairs.

"Julie!" her mother said. "I'm so glad you

slept." She put her arm about her waist. 'This is difficult for everyone, dear. Before you leave for the hospital, I want you to eat something."

"I'm not hungry. Please, Mother, I can't eat now." She looked appealingly at her mother. "Don't ask me to."

"I understand, Julie. But you won't help Dylan by not eating. He's going to depend on your help a great deal."

"I'll eat a bite when I come back, I promise."

"You'll need this," Samuel said, handing her an umbrella. "It's raining."

She took the umbrella, the one she'd received from the Morans on her sixteenth birthday. How long ago that seemed! How wonderfully alive and grown up she'd felt the day she turned sixteen. Now she felt sad and shriveled inside. She glanced gratefully at Samuel as they went outside. She opened the umbrella against the mean drizzle. The gray misty dusk matched her mood. She hoped Dylan's despondent attitude had brightened.

But her hopes were dashed when they entered the darkened space where Dylan lay. His tight lips told her the doctor's prognosis remained the same.

While Samuel lit the lantern, she sat by

the bedside, taking Dylan's hand. "Hello, darling," she murmured.

The strong, dark-haired boy remained motionless, staring at the tent's canvas top. His usual dancing eyes were an intense blue, tinged with bitterness.

She cast about for something to say. Finally, she started brightly, "Dylan, did you know that next Saturday Crocker and his men will attempt to lay ten miles of track?"

He moved his head, eyes blazing. "Why tell me that? Do you think I want to watch those men swing into action for twelve hours when I can't even move my legs?"

"Dylan, I didn't mean. . . ." Her words faded. She wished she hadn't mentioned the bet. How could she have been so insensitive? Distraught, she glanced at Samuel, who tactfully switched to a new topic.

"I've accepted the surveyor's position in Washington," he said. "As soon as the transcontinental is finished, I'll head back East."

Her eyes widened. "You're leaving here?" she asked, astonished.

"Yes, a desk job pays better than anything out in the field," he said, pointedly staring hard at Dylan.

"A desk job!" Dylan snorted. "That wouldn't be for me!"

Her heart ached. That might be the only job Dylan would be suited for now.

Samuel chuckled. "There could be worse things in life. I'm looking forward to it. Then, too, my family is back East." He cleared his throat uneasily. "Uncle Hiram isn't part of our family anymore! Not after what he did!" Samuel looked at Dylan. "I'm really sorry, Dylan. I didn't think Uncle Hiram was capable of such a monstrous thing."

Dylan nodded. "I'm not blaming you, Sam." A brief smile flickered across his parched lips. "Good luck, Sam."

"Well," Samuel said, putting on his hat, "I'd better get out to Wolf's Gate. Your father is waiting for me, Julie. Besides," he winked, "you two might want a little privacy."

" 'Bye, Samuel," Dylan said shortly.

Julie reached out to Samuel, almost afraid to be alone with Dylan, then withdrew her hand. She gave him a small smile instead. "I'll see you later, Samuel."

He looked warmly first at Julie, then Dylan. With a wave he pushed back the tent flap and was gone.

The look between Samuel and Julie wasn't lost on Dylan. "You and Samuel make a good team," he said lightly.

"Of course," she answered, half-teasing. "A team that's rooting for you." She sank down on the edge of the bed. "Dylan, no matter what the doctor says, I know you're going to walk again."

His lip curled in a half-smile. "I didn't know you were such a medical expert, Julie." He shook his head. "I've tried, believe me. There's just no feeling in my leg. It's no use."

"Tomorrow is a new day. I'll bring you a new book to read. *Robinson Crusoe*. You'll like it."

"Isn't Thursday your day to work?" he questioned suspiciously.

"Mother and I trade off all the time," she explained hastily.

"Don't, Julie. Go to work!"

She gulped, fighting back the tears. Had Dylan given up? Or didn't he want to see her? Or both?

Chapter Eighteen

EVERY day for a week Julie had sat by Dylan's bedside, and every day it had been more and more painful. On several occasions he had tried to walk and failed. The last few days he had no longer even tried. It wrenched her heart to see him so quiet and introspective. It was as if he had given up. That day he had asked Samuel to take her to see "Crocker's Pets" try to win their ten thousand dollar bet.

Walking along the curve of the river with Samuel, she felt almost lighthearted. I seemed such a long time since she'd enjoyed a spring day and the birds singing.

"Come on, Julie," Samuel called. "I'll race you to that stump."

"Let's go!" she whooped, tearing out in

front of him. Her ruffled petticoats flew as she held up her skirt to run pell mell through the daisies.

Samuel caught up with her, passed her, and waited by the stump.

In a few seconds she fell into Samuel's outstretched arms. Laughing, she teased. "Samuel, what's come over you? I didn't think I'd ever see the day when you'd dare me to race!" She waggled a finger beneath his nose. "It's not ladylike, you know."

Laughing, he twirled her about. "I've learned a few things from you, Julie. And one thing is to enjoy life. I must have been pretty dull when you first met me."

"Oh, maybe a little," she taunted, "but beneath that sober face is a fun-loving fellow." She grinned. "Why, Samuel, you don't even frown at me when I become too exuberant."

They both laughed. It was almost as if they were two children off on a holiday. Julie felt a twinge of guilt when she thought of Dylan lying despairingly in bed. He said he was looking forward to finishing *Robinson Crusoe,* but she doubted that.

"Julie," Samuel said, turning her about to face him. "I'll miss you when I return to Washington."

"And I'll miss you, Samuel," she said, but she thought of Dylan. She realized she should have stayed with him.

"Your green eyes are glowing." He smiled. "Are you thinking of Dylan?"

"Yes," she confessed. "Oh, Samuel, I wish he could be with us today! He'd love to watch Crocker's men perform."

"I know," Samuel admitted, "but he also wanted us to enjoy the day. So come along. We'll report to Dylan after Crocker forfeits the bet!"

"*If* he forfeits," she replied airily.

When they arrived, the early morning light was breaking over the festive crowd. The nervous Union Pacific executives were already there. Mr. Crocker had planned the track-laying well. If he was successful, the Union Pacific wouldn't be able to challenge his record, for they were only nine and one-half miles from Promontory Point.

Crowds lined both sides of the land where Crocker's men waited, eager to begin. Five trains, each loaded with the material to lay two miles of track, stood on the main line or sidings. Horse-drawn wagons had already dropped the ties into place so that all that was left was the backbreaking job of laying the track.

Suddenly, Crocker, on horseback, rode out, arm upraised. Instantly the engine whistle shrilled. It was seven o'clock, and the crews leaped into action.

Behind Crocker's eight Irish tracklayers

came a crew of Chinese workers, laboring in relays, who graded and ballasted the road-bed. Their wide-brimmed straw hats bobbed up and down, and their wide cotton pants flapped in the wind.

Crocker had deliberately chosen the Irish-men who worked for him to lay track; for if the bet was won he wanted to avert further angry confrontations against his Chinese workers. He knew that using Irishmen to win his bet would soften the blow to Casement's Irish Terriers and their pride.

Julie was caught up in the excitement — the cursing, shouting, clanking of rails, and the rumbling of unloading as she watched the men move forward like a well-oiled precision machine. The rail-layers, four to each side, seized a rail and, running forward, set it in place. The gaugers adjusted them, the spikers swung their sledge hammers, and the rails were fastened to the ties.

Panting and sweating, the rail-layers, refusing substitutes, maintained a steady pace, laying track as fast as a man could walk. The construction crews moved as one man. By dusk, sheer nerve and muscle won out. Crocker's Pets had laid ten miles, with eighteen hundred feet to spare!

Julie, along with the five thousand spectators, cheered until her throat was hoarse. Never had she seen such an incredible feat. Ten miles of track in one day! A sign-post went up, marking the spot called "Victory," just west of Promontory Point.

"I've never seen anything like it," Samuel said enthusiastically, as they returned from shaking hands with the eight track-layers. "All Irishmen: Shay, Kennedy, Sullivan, Joyce, Dailey, Wyatt, Killeen, and Mc-Namara. Dylan will be pleased to hear that!" Samuel exclaimed. "Come on, let's tell him!"

Her eyes sparkled. "He won't believe what we've just seen!"

"No, I guess he won't," Samuel agreed. An awkward silence ensued between them, as they were both struck by the same thought. Perhaps Dylan wouldn't want to hear about such a marvelous exploit. Julie, an ache in her heart, pictured Dylan as he had looked before his accident. Energetic and strong, his graceful body would swing lustily into action, coordinating tirelessly with his fellow workers. And after he had finished the track-laying, he would have exulted in the challenge, his laughter ringing out triumphantly.

As they neared the hospital tent, Julie asked a question, more to break the quiet than for information. "When do you leave for Washington, Samuel?"

"As soon as the big celebration at Promotory Point takes place — sometime next week." He glanced at her and faltered, detaining her with his hand. "Julie," he said haltingly, meeting her eyes, "Dylan is a very proud man. Prepare yourself for the worst. I don't think he'll ever marry you as long as he's bedridden."

"I don't care." She tightened her jaw. "Then I'll be his nurse."

"Dylan won't allow you to sacrifice your life for him," Samuel said, shaking his head. His luminous eyes saddened. "You do realize that, don't you?"

"Dylan is in no position to argue," she retorted smartly, but knew that Dylan was angry when she stayed with him and didn't go to the telegraph office.

"Julie, I know you love Dylan, but the situation has changed." Samuel's questioning look swept over her face. "Are you certain he still loves you?"

"Of course, I'm sure," she said, the words fairly leaping out of her mouth. But her heart was in turmoil, and she wasn't sure. She wasn't sure at all.

"I love you," Samuel said in a low voice, "very much. Dylan has become my best friend, and I love him, too. But I can't help myself!" He smoothed back her auburn curls. "You must know how I feel about you, Julie. I want to marry you and take you to Washington with me." His eyes twinkled. "And you can become an Easterner."

"I couldn't do that," she whispered.

"Hush," Samuel said, holding up his hand.

"I'm not saying you should leave immediately. Stay with Dylan, Julie. He needs you now, but when the railroad camp breaks up, Dylan will be forced to make a decision, and then I'd like you to think of me. I know you could be happy with me. And I know your affection could turn to love." He analyzed her face. "If you don't want to marry right away, you might still come East. Telegraphers are in big demand back there, too. Knowing you, Julie, I'm sure you'll want to work for a while."

"You're understanding, Samuel, and good to me, but. . . ." She fought back tears that threatened to spill over.

"Hush," Samuel said, holding up his hand.

Suddenly Samuel pulled her to him and kissed her. His lips felt warm and sweet.

Reluctantly, she backed away, as shocked at the kiss as at her own response to him. "Samuel," she said, wavering, "I don't know what to say."

His brown eyes were compelling and searching. "Don't say anything. Just listen. You're the only girl for me," he said, inclining his head and smiling. "I don't want to hurt Dylan any more than you do, but I love you. I want you to wear my engagement ring. I'll wait for you, no matter how long it takes." He ran his finger down her cheek. "I only want to see you happy."

"I know you do, Samuel." She was still recovering from his astonishing kiss, still acutely aware of his handsome face and his broad shoulders. Doubt and conflicting emotions swirled in her head.

Abruptly she wheeled about. "Dylan will wonder what's happened to us." Her voice was shaky. She tried to laugh but only managed a faint smile.

"Then we'd better hurry," Samuel said, as if pleased that his kiss had shaken her.

When they arrived at the hospital tent, Dylan eyed both of them. To Julie, it looked as if his enigmatic eyes were filled with suspicion. Quickly she launched into a description of the phenomenal tracklaying event, and although Dylan listened attentively, he kept glancing from her to Samuel.

Later, walking home, Julie didn't ask Samuel in. She needed time to think, time to sort out her feelings.

The next morning Julie went down to breakfast still bewildered by Samuel's kiss. She was torn between her loyalty to Dylan and Samuel's overwhelming love. But of one thing she was certain — she could never leave Dylan. He was her first love and always would be.

"Hi, Julie," Michael greeted her. He was alone at the kitchen table. "Have you heard the news?" His square face broke into a grin.

"No," she said, reaching for the pitcher of

milk, pouring herself a glass, and refilling Michael's. "What's happened?"

"They've captured Hiram and every last one of his men." Michael ate the last of his scrambled eggs, then buttered a second slice of thick bread. "Even confiscated all their Indian regalia. Chief Red Deer was the one who apprehended them. Talk about justice!"

"Thank goodness, the Cheyenne are vindicated."

"You believed in the Indians from the beginning, didn't you?"

"Yes, I did," she said, but there was no pleasure in having Samuel's uncle captured and sent to jail. Absentmindedly, she shook her head when Michael offered her the bread. All at once she leaned over grasping Michael's wrist. "Do you think Dylan will ever walk again?"

Michael's chiseled jawline became even more firm. Hastily he pushed back his chair. "I've got to go to work."

"Do you, Michael?" she repeated stubbornly.

"The doctor says he has a good chance. Sure, I think he'll walk. Eventually." But his words didn't ring true. Bending over, he pecked her on the cheek. "Be patient, little sister." He lifted her chin. "And eat! You're as skinny as a broom handle. You look as if you could use a good night's sleep, too. I've never seen such dark circles under your eyes, or your face so white." He ran his fingers through his thick, red hair, his flinty gray eyes softening. "Will you do that for your big brother?"

She nodded, suddenly smiling at Michael's worried expression.

"Ah," he said happily. "I haven't seen that lovely smile for a long time. It's very becoming!" He moved to the door. "By the way, I'll be late. We're laying track six miles from Promontory Point, and tracks have to be bent for a curve."

"All right, Michael. Be careful," she added as she thought of Dylan. He, too, had left jaunty and bright one morning, but had come back broken and twisted.

After Michael left, Julie sipped her milk, then washed the dishes. She hoped Dylan felt better today. What wonderful news it would be if he'd tell her he had tried to walk. If only he would make an attempt. It wasn't like Dylan to be a quitter.

Hurrying to the hospital tent, she pushed back the flap, and the odor of camphor assailed her nostrils. Dylan, reading, looked up at her entrance and closed his book. "Hi," he said as he gave her his old, cocky grin. Her heart leaped at the sight of his tanned face, dazzling white teeth, and black upraised brows like miniature wings over his bright eyes.

"Dylan!" she exclaimed. "You look marvelous!"

"Well, my head is on a little straighter, if that's what you mean, but my legs are still as useless as two rusted-out rails!"

She hesitated, then plunged ahead. "Rusty rails can still be used." She came forward, smiling. "You need to try your legs every day, Dylan!"

A frown darkened his face. "It's no use. My legs are paralyzed." Then his lip curved back into a smile. "Sit here," he said, patting a place beside him on the bed.

She sank down, yearning once more to hear him call her his darling, his colleen.

"Julie, I've had time to think." He gave a short bark of laughter. "Lots of time. Sam told me about his top job in Washington."

"I know," she murmured, puzzled as to where this was leading.

Dylan brushed back his curls and cleared his throat. "I'll say it plain and clear, Julie. I want you to forget about me and marry Sam!" His blue eyes were as steady and unrelenting as a freshwater stream. "Your future is with Samuel Harper — not with me!"

She couldn't stifle a low cry. "No, Dylan. My place is with you. I'm staying here."

Dylan retained his smile, but his eyes sparked. "There's no reason for you to stay.

I don't want you here. We had a good time together, but now it's over."

Her throat closed as if a giant hand had reached out and clamped it shut. "Dylan, you're just saying this because of. . . ." Words failed her.

"It has nothing to do with my legs!" he said sharply, his mouth firmly set.

"I'll never leave you, Dylan," she said softly.

"Julie, believe me when I tell you it's finished, and take the news gracefully."

Speechless, she stared at him incredulously.

"I wish you and Sam the best," he said cheerfully, reaching for his book in dismissal.

She bit down hard on her lower lip, seething with humiliation and anger. "Perhaps you're right, Dylan," she flared. For an instant she stared at him, but he was engrossed in his book.

Whirling about, she ran blindly, not knowing or caring where she went. Hot tears rolled down her cheeks, and her inner pain was almost more than she could bear.

Chapter Nineteen

FLINGING herself down on the new grass, Julie covered her face with trembling hands and wept aloud. Dylan no longer loved her. It was finished, he'd said. How could something that had been so beautiful be over?

Brushing away her tears, she gulped hard and resolutely sat up. She hugged her knees to her chest, rocking back and forth. So Dylan was arranging her life, telling her she belonged to Samuel. With a shiver of remembrance she felt Samuel's kiss on her lips. If Dylan no longer wanted her, Samuel did! Very well. Her problem was solved. She'd find Samuel and accept his ring. Her whole life would take a different turn than what she'd expected. Her life in Washington, D.C., would be a good one. With Samuel her future wouldn't be uncertain — it would be secure. She'd be able to buy as many pink ruffled dresses as she desired. No longer, though, would riding suits be appropriate. She sighed heavily. Samuel was dependable and had a brilliant career ahead of him. If there were no obstacles to overcome, why did she feel so desolate?

As fond as she was of Samuel, she didn't love him. He didn't cause her heart to pound the way Dylan did. It was *Dylan* she loved, and she wouldn't give him up without a fight.

Slowly she walked back toward town, plotting her strategy to convince Dylan to try to move his legs. She must convince him they belonged to one another and they'd face the future together, no matter what it brought. How could she have even thought of deserting Dylan? A pang of remorse struck her heart. Her pulse picked up. What if he rebuffed her again? How many rejections could she take? No matter, she thought, thrusting out her chin. She had to try. Just as Dylan had to try to walk. But first she'd find Samuel and tell him her decision.

"Hello, Julie! Julie, hello!"

Julie glanced up to see Nell Brannigan, sitting sidesaddle on her great bay. The woman pulled hard on the reins. "You must have been thinking deep thoughts," Nell said with a smile that widened her crimson mouth.

Julie smiled in return. "I was."

"Dylan or Samuel?" she queried, knowingly, arching her thin brows.

"Both," Julie answered, not committing herself. "How are you, Miss Brannigan?"

She shrugged her broad shoulders. Her scarlet riding suit with its double row of shiny black buttons fit her body snugly. "We both have troubles, don't we, Julie? Poor Dylan. Has he made any progress yet?"

"Not yet," Julie responded softly. "He-he's still the same." She couldn't hide the catch in her voice.

"That's too bad, Julie," Nell said in her deep, husky voice. "Any hope?"

"Doctor Nelson gives him a good chance." But a twinge of sadness twisted her heart. She didn't add that Dylan no longer attempted to get out of bed.

"I just came from visiting Hiram at the jailhouse," Nell said. She looked down, arranging her voluminous skirts. When her moist eyes met Julie's again, they were as dazzling as the diamond brooch she wore at her throat. "Hiram dreads the trial," she said tremulously.

Nell really loved Hiram, Julie thought, and marveled at how she could care for such a man.

"He'll stand before the judge next month. The railroad won't look kindly on what he's done!" Nell's voice was almost inaudible.

"You must hate him after what happened to Dylan."

Julie didn't respond, for although she didn't hate Hiram, she did feel a sense of contempt and pity. What a mess he'd made for himself, the Indians, the Union Pacific, and the workers. It had all been so pointless.

Several wagons careened past. Workers yelled out a greeting.

Nell waved exuberantly. "Hi, boys. I'm coming out to see the tracks in a few minutes." She glanced at Julie. "Do you want to ride out to Promontory Point with me? They're building the platform and decorating for the big day tomorrow." She chuckled. "The Red Bull Saloon is bursting with bigwigs from Washington and Sacramento." Her eyes twinkled. "Tomorrow the golden spike will be driven in for the 'wedding' of the two railroads." She threw back her head and laughed. "Would I love to get my hands on that! Solid gold — cast out of twenty-dollar gold pieces. Can you imagine?" She rolled her eyes. "And I wouldn't mind having the silver-headed sledge hammer they'll be using, either!" Again her jubilant laughter filled the air.

"It will be something to see," agreed Julie.

"Ride out with me," Nell urged.

"No, I need to find Samuel," she said, dreading the confrontation.

"Samuel's at Hiram's house," Nell said, tossing back the veil from her smart derby hat. "I'll see you at the ceremony tomorrow."

Julie brightened. "I'll be there. And, Miss Brannigan," she called, "maybe Hiram will get off with a light sentence."

"I hope so!" Nell replied fervently. "I'm grateful he didn't kill anyone!"

No, just maimed and destroyed, Julie thought bitterly, but she choked her words back, even managing a smile for Nell as she waved good-bye.

On the way to Hiram Harper's house, Julie reflected on the Golden Spike Ceremony. It would be thrilling, for she and Mother had been selected to send the telegraph message back to Washington. A magnetic ball was in place on the Capitol Building's dome and was attached to the telegraphic circuit so that it would fall on the electric impulse when the first blow was struck on the golden spike.

In fact, every city in the country awaited the message so that parades could begin, bands could play, and festivities start. A feeling of pride surged through her. She was to be part of a momentous historical event!

As she hurried along Ogden's main street, she passed a throng of visitors from the East.

Men in black frock coats, tall hats, and cravats escorted their elegant ladies dressed in silks and ostrich plumes. However, at present, her thoughts were on Samuel, and she scarcely saw the happy, chattering crowd.

Standing on Hiram's porch, she paused. How could she tell Samuel? She knocked. Lifting her head a notch, she was determined to be straightforward and to the point.

But when Samuel flung open the door and she saw his face lighting up at her presence, her resolve weakened.

"What a pleasant surprise, Julie. Come in." He opened the door wider.

Entering, she glanced around at the furniture covered with cloth.

Samuel, shirt sleeves rolled up, took her shawl. "I'm packing a few of the personal things Uncle Hiram wanted," he explained, holding out a chair. "Sit down. I'll fix us a cup of coffee."

"None for me," she said quickly, holding up her hand. The sooner she got this over with, the better she'd feel. "Go ahead with what you're doing Samuel."

He opened a leather valise and put in a moustache cup, shaving mug, shaving brush, and comb. "He'll need this," Samuel said, chuckling and holding up a bar of soap. "You know, Julie, Uncle Hiram's a very fastidious man."

"I'm not surprised. Samuel, you even have a little of your uncle in you when it comes to being well-groomed," she said, her smiling eyes glancing over his clean-shaven, good-looking features. He wore black twill trousers and a gleaming white shirt. His wavy hair, thick and shiny, was cut just below his ears.

"As long as the comparison stops there," he said with a broad smile. "I certainly don't want any of his scheming ways to rub off on me."

"Not you, Samuel. I can see your future now. You'll be admired and move up the promotion ladder fast. I'd like to see what you do in your career, but I won't be with you. I'll be here!"

Samuel dropped Hiram's hairbrush, staring at her. "Does that mean what I think it does?"

Slowly she nodded. "I'm on my way to the hospital. This time Dylan is going to listen to me. I have no intention of ever leaving him again."

"I see," Samuel said, busily rearranging the items in the valise. "Then, despite Dylan's wishes, I'll be traveling to Washington alone."

"Yes, Samuel, but," she grasped his wrist, forcing him to look at her, "I'll always have a special place in my heart for you."

He gazed longingly into her eyes. "You're

so beautiful, Julie, with your red hair tumbling about your lovely face," he said, smiling. "And just when I was becoming accustomed to your free spirit!"

"A spirit that wears better in the West than it would in the East," she countered. "Oh, look, Samuel, you understand as well as I do that I'd be uncomfortable at all the formal affairs you'd be invited to. And because of me, you'd be uncomfortable, too."

"Never!" he whispered.

"Samuel, you'll find an elegant girl with perfect manners. She'll be a source of pride and be able to entertain and help you in your career. That's what you need!"

"I'll always love you, Julie." And although his gaze was warm and wistful, she felt he didn't protest her decision as much as she'd thought he would. No, it was obvious she wasn't leaving Samuel with a broken heart. Cracked a little, maybe, but not broken. Quickly she brushed his cheek with her lips and moved to the door.

"Dylan's a lucky fellow!" he called after her. "Good-bye, sweet Julie."

She hurried out, breathing hard. It hadn't been as difficult as she had thought, but she was glad it was over!

Now she would have to face Dylan, but her buoyant happiness knew no bounds. To see Dylan was her fondest desire. She picked up her skirts, running. She was confident in her love for Dylan. And with sudden clarity, she knew he loved her, too.

Arriving at the hospital tent, she threw back the flap and stopped. Her throat closed as she tightly gripped the canvas. Dylan, his back to her, was standing! He began to place one foot in front of the other! Wordlessly, she observed him as he walked, using two canes for support. Her heart soared with joy. He could use his legs! Tears of dazzling happiness spilled down her face.

Putting her hand to her mouth, she silently watched this glorious moment. Her breathing was as light as a thistledown. She didn't want to break Dylan's concentration as he moved laboriously around the room. How she yearned to rush to his side and enfold him in her arms.

All at once, no longer able to restrain herself, she rushed toward him with her hands outstretched. On the way forward, however, her skirts brushed against a small table, upsetting a medicine bottle which shattered on the wooden floor.

Dylan whirled about, his canes flying out from under him, and he went crashing to the floor.

"Dylan! Darling!" she shouted with concern, dashing to his side.

Grimacing in pain, Dylan pushed himself up on his elbows, his dark eyes glowering. "Stand back!" he barked.

She halted, not daring to advance, even though her heart cried out to him.

"Get out of here, Julie!" He stared at her with eyes that glowed like deep turquoise. "Where's Samuel?" he asked abruptly. "Go to him. We've discussed this before. We're finished!"

Stubbornly, she shook her head, brushing back her tears. "We're not finished, only beginning." Despite his warning she ran to him. "You can't shut me out any longer," she said, her voice breaking. "I prayed for this moment." She flung herself down beside him, cradling him in her arms. "To see you walking again makes this the happiest day of my life!"

Dylan, his curls in disarray and almost touching his thick black brows, stiffened. "Get out," he commanded between clenched teeth. Then his voice broke and his eyes softened. "Please."

"Never," she whispered, her arms tightening about his neck. "I'm staying here, and you won't get rid of me this time!"

Suddenly his taut body went slack, and he buried his face in her hair. "Oh, me darling Julie, how I've longed to hold you in my arms. To kiss you. To tell you I love you. But

I couldn't. Don't you see? I didn't want your pity. Or to tie you to a cripple for the rest of your life, especially when you had the opportunity to marry Sam."

Holding his face between her hands, she gazed deep into his eyes. "What a fool you are, Dylan O'Kelly! Did you think I'd give you up so easily?"

A soft chuckle caught in his throat. Sitting up, he returned her look of love. "Ain't it grand, me darling?"

"It's ever so grand," she repeated. "Now you're a railroad man again, and," she laughed, blissfully happy, "my Irish Terrier again!"

Dylan enfolded her in his arms. His blue eyes were bright with unshed, sparkling tears. He kissed her, and she could feel his heart beat. At last she was where she belonged!

Chapter Twenty

THE next afternoon, Julie, still deliriously happy over Dylan's progress, sat at her telegrapher's bench alongside her mother. Directly in front of them was Mr. Shilling, the head telegrapher from Ogden. How exciting to be part of the Golden Spike Ceremony about to take place. Promontory Point would live in history, even though it was not the most beautiful place for the event. The town was on a high plateau with only a few scrub cedars and sagebrush. Great Salt Lake, a lovely contrast of blue, lay one thousand feet below.

Crowds lined both sides of the tracks and jammed the excursion trains on the siding. The Chinese in blue with their basket hats, the Mormons in black, and the ladies and gentlemen from the East and West who swarmed onto the rails from their decorated coaches, all made a colorful sight. Workers, Indians, Mexicans, mountain men, and ranchers drifted all along the line.

Craning her neck, Julie could see every tie had been laid except one. A place had been reserved to put the last tie in the exact center of the main track. Then the transcontinental railroad would be complete!

Along the main line from the west chuffed the Central Pacific's engine, Jupiter, a wood-burner. It was an impressive sight with its bright crimson and gold trim and balloon smokestack. Jupiter's engineer stopped at the break in the rails, almost nose-to-nose with Engine Number One-nineteen of the Union Pacific, a coal-burner. Engine One-nineteen, in stark contrast to the Jupiter, was painted dark green and black with a straight coffee-grinder stack. But even though Number One-nineteen was somber in color, its brass fittings were dazzingly polished. Both trains were decorated with red, white, and blue bunting and flags that snapped smartly in the breeze.

The Twenty-first Military Band struck up a lively march when Governor Stanford met Dr. Durant of the Central Pacific and General Dodge of the Union Pacific. Each was carrying a silver sledge-hammer, which glinted in the sun.

Julie's heart beat faster when the last tie, made of polished California laurel, was brought up. Newspapermen took notes. Photographers, their large box cameras set on tripods, squeezed rubber bulbs, taking pictures of the locomotives and dignitaries.

Speeches were made, and the jostling crowd grew restless. At last the tie, bound with silver, was carried forward. It had a silver plate on which was engraved:

THE LAST TIE LAID ON THE COMPLETION OF THE PACIFIC RAILROAD, MAY 10, 1869.

Next, the two rails were carried forward, the north rail by Union Pacific Irish and the south rail by Crocker's Pets, the Chinese. As the two groups ran forward with their rails, Charles Savage, the noted photographer, placed his camera in position to catch the act. Someone called out, "Now's the time, Charlie. Shoot!"

Finally, Reverend Todd stepped up to the platform and a hush of anticipation fell over the crowd. Bowing their heads, they listened to his short prayer.

"Are you ready?" Rosie asked, her dark hair framing her jovial face and her fingers poised over the telegraph key.

"Ready, Mother," Julie answered, breathless with suspense.

"Then tap out your message."

Julie clicked the key, relaying this message to Chicago:

> WE'RE DONE PRAYING. THE SPIKE IS
> ABOUT TO BE PRESENTED.

Telegraph wires were coiled around the silver hammers so that the four spikes driven in could be heard all over the country.

Julie quickly glanced around and spied Samuel with Dylan sitting on the back end of a horse-drawn cart. Dylan grinned at her and blew a kiss. She did the same. Samuel waved, seemingly happy for both of them. What a marvelous sight to see her Gandy Dancer recuperating.

"Julie," her mother cautioned, "pay attention. The last spike is about to be driven in!"

Julie flashed her message:

> ALL READY NOW.

An instant later the silver hammer came down, and she clicked out one word:

> DONE!

The golden spike had been driven home, uniting the country by iron rails from coast to coast. The engines inched forward, whistles shrieking. The two engineers stood on the cowcatchers and broke champagne bottles, wetting the rails with sparkling wine. When they shook hands, the band blared even louder to drawn out the crowd's roar. Julie remembered the verse Bret Harte, the San Francisco writer, had composed in anticipation of this event:

> What was it the Engines said,
> Pilots touching — head to head,
> Facing on the single track,
> Half a world behind each back?

All at once Julie was startled to see people swarming over both trains and clambering into the engines. They leaned out of the cabs, waving wildly and posing for photographers.

Then, as if a conductor had stepped forth to conduct, the onlookers moved together and broke into song. The sweet strains of "Auld Lang Syne" floated on the chill air. Tears welled up in Julie's eyes. So much good feeling and happiness surrounded her. Could life be any better? And tonight the festivities would continue when all Promontory Point gathered to celebrate the occasion.

Ready to leave, Julie looked for Dylan but saw him being helped by Dr. Nelson and Jack Casement. They moved slowly in the direction of the hospital. Her pulse fluttered erratically. She hoped nothing was wrong. Now that the railroad was completed most men were unemployed. As a result the saloons were overflowing. Thanks to the Casements, though, many workers had been sent free of charge back East. Dylan had once been Jack Casement's best worker. Why was he talking so intently to Dylan? She fervently hoped he didn't plan to fire Dylan. That would be the worst thing that could happen to him now.

Samuel hurried over to their telegraph station, which was already being dismantled. "May I escort home the two most beautiful women in Utah?"

Rosie chuckled, glancing at Julie. "Samuel, you're as bad as Dylan with your blarney — and you're not even Irish!"

Samuel grinned, his classically handsome features filled with warmth. "Well, how about it? May I take you home?"

"Escort Julie," said Rosie. "I need to supervise the proper placement of the telegraph at the depot." Her eyes twinkled. "I'll see you at the party, though. And, Samuel, I've packed a basket for your train trip home tomorrow."

"Mmm — my mouth is watering already — thank you, Rosie."

After she'd gone, Samuel turned to Julie. "Mademoiselle," he said, inclining his head and holding out his arm, "may I?"

Julie, matching his mood, took his elbow, giving him a sweet smile. "You may." She stepped high, skirting several mud puddles.

Samuel looked at Julie. "Will Dylan be coming by?"

"I'll meet him at the party. He's not to try to walk too much yet."

Sam patted her hand. "It's so great to see Dylan walking again and have him so vibrantly alive!"

"It is, isn't it?" she said, smiling as if an inner light glowed from within. "Samuel," she asked, "do you know what Jack Casement wanted?"

Samuel shrugged. "I don't know. Doc Nelson did warn Dylan that he either had to rest or miss tonight's party." He barked a laugh. "You know Dylan! Would he miss a chance to have a good time?"

A slight crease furrowed her brow. "It would be just like Dylan to overdo. With him there are no half-way measures."

Samuel stopped, touching her elbow. "I won't be staying late tonight, Julie. I'll be leaving on the eight o'clock train tomorrow morning." He paused, eyes locking with hers. "If you and Dylan ever come East, I want you to stay with me."

Her laugh tinkled on the brisk air. "Samuel, you're sweet. We'll all miss you!"

He tilted up her chin and studied her face as if fixing her image in his mind. "I'll never forget you, Julie." For a moment she thought he was going to kiss her, but instead he abruptly turned, calling over his shoulder, "See you at the party."

Her heart went out to Samuel, wishing she could erase the sadness she'd seen in his eyes.

But that night, dressing for the banquet, she thought only of Dylan. Wriggling into her new pleated, ivory-colored gown, she felt like a princess. Tiny seed pearls decorated her scooped neckline and green velvet ribbons cascaded down the front. The pale dress made her hair an even more vivid auburn, highlighting hidden golden streaks. Gazing into the mirror, she put on her grandmother's pearls and the pierced pearl earrings that her mother had lent her. She picked up a lace snood to tuck in her abundant hair, but at the last moment tossed it back on the dresser. Because Dylan liked her hair flowing over her smooth shoulders, that was the way she'd wear it.

One tiny flaw bothered her in all the recent wonderful happenings. Maybe two. First of all, she had to worry about Jack Casement's plans for Dylan, if any, and second, she couldn't marry Dylan, at least not right away. Her parents wanted her to wait until she was at least seventeen before marrying. That was almost a year away! She wouldn't go against her parent's wishes. They'd been marvelous. Why should she break their hearts by running away and getting married? No, this was something she and Dylan needed to work out. She hoped he would be understanding.

That evening the hall was ablaze with colorful lanterns, its rafters hung with banners, flags, and silver ribbons.

Dylan, seated by the door, slowly got to his feet, leaning on a cane, at the sight of her. He looked handsome and debonair in his brown belted corduroy suit and white shirt. "Julie!" he exclaimed, his eyes shining with love. "I was waiting for you." He smiled, lightly touching her hair. "You look grand!"

She was pleased at his obvious pleasure, but she didn't exactly know how to tell him they couldn't marry immediately, especially with couples coming in, greeting them, and the band playing.

Samuel came over and said cheerfully, "I've saved two places at the banquet table, unless, of course," he smiled widely, "you two would rather be alone."

"Samuel," Dylan said, clapping his friend on the back, "we'll be proud to sit with you. Listen, me boy, Julie and I are going to get married. Will you be my best man?" Using only one cane, Dylan stood straight and proud, beaming at Julie.

Julie caught her breath, not knowing what

to say. She must talk to Dylan alone. Blushing, she studied her green satin slippers, not daring to meet his eyes.

"Just name the day and place," Samuel declared, "and I'll be there! Now, I've got to get back before our chairs are taken."

As soon as Samuel left, Jack Casement entered. His dark eyes lit up when he glimpsed Dylan. "Have you told Julie the news?" he inquired gruffly.

"No, sir, I haven't." He gave Julie a sidelong glance. "But I'm about to."

"Do it!" ordered Jack, quickly walking by.

"Tell me what?" Julie asked, her eyes widening in puzzlement.

"Let's sit over there in the corner," Dylan said.

Julie led the way, threading her way through the milling crowds. Everyone drank champagne, repeating toast after toast to the transcontinental railroad.

Seated on the wicker divan, she turned to Dylan and blurted out, "First, *I* have something to tell you." Her pulse raced with her thoughts. She didn't want to be separated from him, but there was no other way. She had to return with her parents.

"Dylan," she began, then hesitated. "I — I. . . ."

"Yes?" he said. A probing query came into his eyes as he waited for her to proceed. "What is it, me darlin' girl?" He gave her a sharp look. "You still want to marry me, don't you?" His voice was low and anxious.

"Oh, yes, Dylan, but . . . but not right now. I'll be going back to Denver with my parents. They've asked me to wait for at least a year."

"A year, is it?" Dylan said in a teasing, amused tone. He took her hand and held it in a warm clasp.

His hand felt strong and protective. But why didn't he say something else?

Finally he half-turned, facing her. "Would you believe Jack Casement has hired me to go with him as his construction boss?"

Her heart thudded. "Where?" she questioned, wondering how she could bear to be apart from him.

He laughed with sheer joy. "To Denver! We'll be building the Denver Pacific to Cheyenne."

Unbelieving, she stared at him. "You mean you're. . . ?"

"Exactly, me sweet colleen. I'll be living on Jack's construction train right outside Denver. A year's wait means I can save money. I've already invested in the Kansas Pacific, and if it pays off like I think it will, we'll be rich!" He winked. "Besides, I'll get a big raise in my new job!"

"Plus," she bantered, "my salary as a telegrapher."

"So, you're going to work, are you?"

"Certainly. After all, it's for the railroad!"

He shrugged his shoulders in mock resignation. "I knew I'd have trouble when I got myself involved with a redhead. Ah, Julie," he said, "whatever you want is all right with me." He held her in the circle of his arms.

"Dylan!" she said humorously, pulling back in false indignation. "What will all these people think?"

"They'll think," he said seriously, "that I'm the luckiest railroad man in the U.S.A."

"But. . . ."

"Hush, Julie," he said. He leaned forward and tenderly kissed her lips.

She felt her heart surge with delight. The year she had been worried about was now a year she looked forward to. And with Dylan by her side, she could face anything!

Coming next from Sunfire: RACHEL, a beautiful girl who emigrates from Europe to find freedom, and love, in America. But will she be the same after she survives a raging fire? And when two boys — one who clings to the old customs of Europe, one who is eager to be a modern American — win her heart, which one will Rachel choose?